THE PASSED ON

WILLIAM KERRIGAN

ISBN 978-1-942946-14-4

This book is so full of Ted Tayler stuff that it has to be dedicated to him. Thanks again, Edward William Tayler, for everything.

The witchcraft of sleep divides with truth the empire of our lives.

Ralph Waldo Emerson, "Demonologie"

CHAPTER ONE

I had the house to myself when I got back from my morning Yoga class at the YMCA in Lassiter Springs. Cheyenne and her mother Valentina Griswold were probably out riding. Her father Ben was probably crafting silver-trimmed saddles in his shop in the barn. I'm the husband and son-in-law, Mike Buckman, and I am a camera among other things, so I took the opportunity to track through our ramshackle home and record one last reel of memory images. It was Friday. On Monday Cheyenne and I would be moving into a rented bungalow on the outskirts of New Aarhus while a contractor and his crew began major renovations on this house.

Back at the purchasing stage, just before our marriage, both of us despised the shabby black and white chessboard linoleum in the kitchen, the sorry avocado appliances, the embarrassing birds and branches on the dining room wallpaper, the cheapo knotty pine bookshelves lining the home office, the garish purple-and-gold cathouse decor of the master bedroom, the hopelessly unfashionable pink tiles in the master bathroom. All eyesores, all the pits. The boorish tastes of an obsolete world.

Now, however, we had lived here for six

months. Our marriage had begun in this rundown, laughable house. Where before there had been eyesores, now there were charms. The life force in Cheyenne's brown eyes had touched the wallpaper's wrens and sparrows. When she walked out of the shower in a slick coat of water, the pink and black patterns of the bathroom tile seemed the ideal backdrop. Entering the kitchen, I remembered the evening Shy (as she's called for short) introduced my libido to its new touchstone in donning a lime green apron bought that afternoon to harmonize with our avocado range, dishwasher, and fridge. The terrible appliance color had earned a place in our erotic history. I thought about the house as it was now, with all its embarrassments, and the house as it would soon be, gutted and rethought, modern, full of art and character. Don't get me wrong. The new home would be welcome in a thousand enduring ways. But I would miss the embarrassments, now linked forever with the happiest days of my life.

My first attempt at matrimony hadn't gone so well. After taking my Master's Degree in Film Studies at Columbia University's School of the Arts, I accepted a highly desirable job with the American Film Institute in Hollywood. At one of their events I met Carolyn Nast, a hotshot Hollywood producer on her way up. We dated. We clicked. We shared candid thoughts about films and the business that made them. We took a trip to New York to meet her mother. Then, without much more of a prelude than that, we married. There was nothing shocking or unexpected about our new status. Being married seemed a mildly more convenient form of dating.

We continued with our careers. Carolyn spent most of her time planning movies, which is to say, arranging conferences and meetings with breakfasts, lunches, and dinners in between. Then came the actual making of the damn movie from shoot to premiere. If you described the planning as a cyclone of activity, what would you call the actual making? A Category 5 on the Saffir-Simpson hurricane scale? There were crises to weather, fateful decisions to make, trying egos to manage, the rigid demands of art to balance against the rigid demands of commerce. Then, when the movie was done at last, the money spent and the decisions made, the winners uncertainly grateful and the losers nursing their grudges, there was the next movie to plan. I helped out here and there, made the occasional suggestion, stayed awake for long talks about how to bust a logjam in casting or make some rigid asshole writer see the light. But mostly I pursued my own career as a film scholar.

I had the shock of my life, as they say, when I

walked in on Carolyn paying serious attention with soft tissue inside her mouth to the gender marker of one of her most ambitious male assistants. It turned out that, unknown to me, she had been doing the nasty with lots of lucky guys throughout our nearly three year marriage. I was quite possibly the most famous cuckold in all Hollywood: the funny old-fashioned kind as opposed to the new sort who checked the Infidelity Expected box on their prenup; the blind as they come variety, that honestly had no idea. Tinsel Towners in the know (nearly everybody, if you judged by self-assessment) had been laughing behind my back from the day I married her.

The divorce settlement left me a rich man, but feeling the more contemptible for it. I had to get out of Los Angeles. Taking an indefinite leave of absence from the AFI, I went north to the Central Coast of California, the rural area around Las Sombras and Lassiter Springs, where I met Shy and became embroiled in one hell of a ghost story. When the Ghost Killers, as Billy Steele, Solomon Barlow, Cheyenne and myself came to call ourselves, had in the end rid the world of the ghosts of Black Ash Canyon (more on that later), Cheyenne Herrera Griswold and Michael Wilbur Buckman decided to tie the knot.

Maybe I pay too much attention to the endless

info-buzz put out by our expert-obsessed culture, but I expected my first marriage to interfere with the second. Didn't first marriages always do that? Wouldn't some "unresolved issue" come back to haunt me?

No, not really. Not at all!

For this was a different order of connection from the last try. This was it. With Carolyn there was in the first place never leisure enough to explore each other. She always felt the pressure of the next meeting to arrange, the next director to lure, the next script to doctor. We hadn't even considered a real honeymoon. To Shy and me, on the other hand, interaction was a shared rapture. Nothing trumped our togetherness. Nothing was more fun or more completing. This was love, and there was no hurry up in it. If you didn't feel like confronting a potentially ticklish matter today, there was always tomorrow or next week.

I felt it to be a miracle, arranged for our benefit, that Shy had steered clear of marriage through her late twenties. There had been partners. She knew men, and she had felt great affection, maybe love, for some of them. But she could not become an adult until she had finished being a child, could not make her own way in life until the curses on her very existence had been put to rest.

Something was wrong in her mother's soul. She

had always known that in some fashion. She remembered from childhood the alarming games Valentina would play. Little Cheyenne would ask what was in her mother's purse. "A knife" was the answer. A short chain of questions led to her mother's revelation of the purpose of the knife in the purse: to kill the child. Then Valentina would laugh gaily, hugging her confused, apprehensive daughter. Today Cheyenne knew these word rituals derived from the everyday games of nineteenth-century children. But she had grown up with the suspicion that ordinary reality was continuous with a semi-secret world of violence and perversion.

Cheyenne tried to understand this lurid behavior as mere eccentricity. These were just violent thoughts that had found outlets in a game, not intentions really meant. In recent years Val had begun talking in disconcerting ways about death. "I'm not sure whether I'm alive or not," she would say, her dark inward-focused eyes framed by her white hair. "But if it were my choice, I would choose dead. It's embarrassing to be alive, don't you think? The living should be ashamed of themselves, holding onto the world so greedily." Doctors spoke of dementia, senility, early Alzheimer's.

For several years, Shy put her career on hold, leaving a good job in a ritzy Montecito gallery to return to the Griswold Ranch in Black Ash Canyon with the twin hopes of comforting her mother and preventing her father from shouldering the burden all by himself. Last year, soon after I rented one of the cottages on the Griswold Ranch, it came to light that Valentina had been possessed from her early teens by the vengeful spirit of her grandfather. He had directed the teenager to murder her own parents, then prompted the old woman to exile their ghosts. This was part of the doozy of a ghost story I mentioned earlier. From Shy's point of view, our successful termination of her grandfather's ghost cleared the path to love and marriage.

But the Black Ash Canyon case had exposed certain differences between Cheyenne and myself that I expected to remain trouble spots in our marriage. A fair degree of intellectual compatibility did not extend to God. Did the return of the dead to this earth imply an afterlife? A deity? Shy was far more open to this kind of speculation than I was. Discussing the subject one evening on the back porch of this house, we decided in an ecumenical manner that we would always take our ghosts as they came. God would be left out of things unless he was in them from the beginning, in what a spirit wanted to accomplish or how he went about it.

The matter of Shy's parents was addressed

without friction. It was evident to both of us that they could no longer manage alone. Separated from her ghost, Valentina had become less eerie and oracular. But she was also more imperious, more apt to complain and demand. Clearly she was struggling to find a workable rationale for life now that her demanding ghost was no longer stealing into her mind and giving her a reason to keep it in order. The Griswolds gratefully accepted our offer, and moved onto our new ranch. Their property in Black Ash Canyon was leased to long-time tenant Solly Barlow, who had been renting their so-called "Creekside Chalet" for the last twenty years. Barlow, a fellow Ghost Killer, decided to remain in the Chalet and outfit the main ranch house for corporate retreats and family vacations.

Ben was optimistic. In the days after the ghost's demise he often expressed his joy at being given a second chance at the back end of life to recover the love he and Valentina had enjoyed in their early years. He was eager to shed some responsibilities, freeing time and energy for the job of renewing his marriage. But I suspected that Ben had never been the most important man in Valentina's life. For her, the experience of being haunted intimately for over fifty years had devalued to some extent all merely human relations. Ben could touch her, converse with her. But he could not slip into her thoughts, know immediately their degree of purity or impurity, and try to shape them to his will. Valentina missed the intimate tussles of possession.

The whole matter of Valentina's lost personal ghost led eventually to my doorstep. For one of the major surprises of our dealings with Herrera was the revelation that, unknown to me, I also had been inhabited by a grandfather's ghost since childhood. He was Wilbur Arlington Buckman, who married three times (unusual in his day) and made his living from an antique store on Geary St. in San Francisco. Like a fortune-hunting sea captain from centuries past, Wilbur crisscrossed the world in search of art and antiques, authoring a small collection of travel journals with titles such as *Paris Provinciality* and *Adventures in British Junk*. In old age he moved to the country inn my parents ran in the coastal mountains between Paso Robles and the beach towns. Grampa Wilbur and I became great pals. I loved him deeply in those days. But I had no idea that his ghost had taken up residence in the wells and shafts of my mind, the spirit was so quiet.

Grampa Wilbur almost always kept to himself, like a passenger on a busy train. He did not issue commands. He did not want to be the engineer or

the conductor or the mogul owning the railroad.
Though deeply curious about our destination and
the evolving amenities of the coaches, he was
mostly content just to sit, ride, and stare out the
window. Valentina's tyrannical ghost had of
course insisted on managing everything. That's
how I knew from the first that Valentina was
grasping at straws when she became curious about
Wilbur, asking me whether the spirit manifested
himself to me at a particular time each day, how I
prepared my mind for these visits, whether our
relationship would continue in a new form after
my death, and similar questions presupposing a
whole spectrum of slightly perverse chumminess
that I had never explored with Grampa Wilbur.

I knew where this was headed, and indeed, she
finally got to the point. One evening as the family
was enjoying a bottle of wine before dinner, Valentina asked me point blank whether my grandfather
would be interested in visiting her. She wanted it
to be a formal date. "My Silver King," she said,
using one of her earliest names for the Herrera
ghost, "came later and later as I moved through
life. At the end I could count on him at 2 AM. But
perhaps Mr. Buckman would rather visit earlier?
Ben and I have always slept in separate bedrooms.
Why, come to think of it, Mr. Buckman could drop
in after dinner tonight." Wilbur and I were com-

municating a bit more often since I had become aware of his occupation. We had a mental conversation right after my exchange with Valentina.

"I'm certain about this, Michael. I won't do it. Like Blanche DuBois, she depends too much on the kindness of strangers. She'll try to seduce me into moving in. I'll refuse, and that will break her heart. She'll collapse in grief. Though blamed on me, it will be the old Herrera grief all over again. That's what she wants—never to relinquish the Herrera grief, and die a martyr to her precious Silver King."

"You could be right," I thought in his direction. *"But you realize that I'm going to be blamed for her disappointment. Ben and Shy may think that I failed to represent the full extent of Valentina's neediness to you. They may even think that I wanted you all to myself."*

Wilbur's mind was made up. *"Believe me, I see the extent of her neediness. As for us—well, we've gotten to be a habit. We get on pretty well, don't we, keeping to our own affairs?"*

"I just hate to stir up unnecessary trouble in my marriage. Couldn't you drift over to the guest house and sit in her mind for a while? Enough for her to feel once again the thrill of having a ghost in her brain? That might be all she wants, for crying out loud."

"Sorry, but nothing doing."

"I don't like the idea of my mother-in-law envying me."

"Live with it."

I knew at once our chat was over. My mind re-acquainted itself with the yawning silence customarily surrounding its thoughts. Wilbur had ended with a joke.

Valentina, when I told her the next day of Wilbur's refusal, walked off to her quarters for a good long cry. I looked uncertainly at Cheyenne, but she flashed me an understanding smile. "I don't blame him. Any ghost calling on my mother is in for a warehouse of baggage."

My marriage was on a roll. Nothing seemed able to waylay us. Feared rough patches and detours became flower gardens bordering the road and scenting our passage.

I microwaved half a cup of coffee and carried it to my favorite chair on the back patio. The early summer morning remained overcast, a captive of what they called "June Gloom" all along the California coast. The phenomenon had nothing to do with nature's moodiness, but was just a simple matter of the marine layer moving inland a few miles. We were fifteen miles from the coast, with misty skies that ought to be overlooking seascapes.

Before me lay the reasons we had purchased this property. The house was perched on a hill. I looked out on the edge of twenty acres of gentle golden hills, dotted with clumps of gnarled California oaks. Above them, in the distance, dark blue in the morning shadows, rose the taller, craggy peaks of the Santa Ynez Mountains dividing our valley from Santa Barbara. A seasonal creek wound through the land. To my left, just behind our house, was a small fruit orchard. To my right stood a red barn fronted by corrals. Past the barn, fifty yards from the main house, was the property's newest building, a two-bedroom guest cottage with tasteful finishes that had proven to be an ideal home for Valentina and Ben Griswold. My in-laws were close to us, part of our daily lives, but also at a comfortable distance.

On horseback Cheyenne and her mother appeared at the crest of the hill behind our house and started down its gradual slope. Valentina was riding her beautiful old palomino Thunderbolt. She had a dark leathery face framed by wings of white hair parted in the middle. Shy, on her chestnut stallion Rex, wore her white straw cowgirl hat, from which brown locks streamed down. I took a good long husbandly look at my wife, especially at her bottom jiggling comfortably against the saddle.

At that moment the phone in my pocket went off. The screen identified the caller as Billy Steele. I clicked him in. "Hey, Billy. Hang on for a bit, will you? I'm going to take this in the office." I stood and waved hello to the ladies. When I had their attention, I pointed at the phone and then toward the house. Shy saluted me and I waved back.

In the study Billy and I chatted a bit before getting down to business. The new Ghost Killers team had performed so well in the Black Ash Canyon case that Billy believed we had serious market potential as supernatural investigators able to rid our clients of unwanted otherworldly pests. A decade back, after two years at a local college, Steele had opened a business in Las Sombras peddling the services of the original Ghost Killers, who were made up of high school friends sharing the boss's bottomless fascination with the occult. That business had folded in a couple of years. But Billy felt certain that the new Ghost Killers, if properly publicized, could attract customers from around the world.

We had everything we needed, as Steele understood the supernatural realm. The four current Ghost Killers were all exceptionally honest and intelligent, all skeptical by nature, all convinced that a good default attitude toward ghosts was to eliminate them from this earth rather than validate their presence with our pity and empathy. A born leader, Billy possessed deep knowledge and strong opinions about the techniques and equipment employed by conventional ghost hunters. Moreover, he had a good feel for spirit doings. His hypotheses about motives and means usually proved sound in the end. I was a tenacious researcher who had internalized in graduate film school the ethos of real scholarship, and in partnership with Wilbur could also be an effective warrior. Solly, with his background in petroleum engineering, had concocted the unique method we used to dispose of the Herrera ghost. It was this above all, Billy declared at the time, that would make our team famous in the world of paranormal investigation. Solly also had a down-to-earth disposition that kept Billy and me from losing ourselves in lofty speculations. Cheyenne, being Valentina's daughter, had been familiar with ghosts from an early age. Playing in her home had sparked young Steele's initial interest in the supernatural. Her supple understanding of the Seven Deadly Sins had helped me recover from two traumatic invasions by Herrera.

Besides, as Billy once said to me man to man, every good team needs women to make sure that all sides of an issue have a fair hearing and outcomes benefit as many as possible. Someone had written a book arguing that these goals characterized female moral thinking in particular. Though

Billy maintained her research was totally bonkers, he also thought the thesis was probably correct, at least for the time being. If women got to thinking that being fair to everyone was their unique business, things might change in a hurry.

Pleased with his new Ghost Killers and hoping to unlock their commercial potential, Billy Steele spent two months writing a pithy account of our maiden case. The book, called *Surveyor of Hell: The Long Haunting of Black Ash Canyon*, was snapped up by the Gray Phantom Press in Santa Cruz and hurried into print several months ago. Reviewers were mostly enthusiastic. Certain of the more liberal occult publications and websites found the method invented to kill the Herrera ghost inhumane and environmentally unprogressive, but said so in such a manner that their readers became eager to experience for themselves the cowboy swagger and political insouciance of the new Ghost Killers team. The book sold, at first through occult bookstores, Wiccan shops, gaming emporiums, and small independent merchandizers stocking objects related to fantasy and magic. Later, as the word spread, large internet distributors began to move the title. Daedalus bought five hundred copies to sell through its mail order catalogue. Gray Phantom Press planned a second edition by the end of the year. Billy Steele had a best-seller on his hands—and more business than he knew what to do with.

We were certainly the only ghost investigation team in the world that could boast of two best-selling authors. My own exploration of a neurotic bond characteristically forged by female performers—I called it *Adoration or Else: Disturbed Actresses and Their Audience*—had been on the trade lists for months and was still selling at a brisk clip. The Ghost Killers topped the field in Literacy Power. Now, whether the people hiring ghost investigators were the sort to appreciate Literacy Power—that was another matter. They might prefer expertise with electronic field meters or whatever. Those ghost teams on TV seemed challenged to read their dials, not to mention books.

I told Billy early on that, although Cheyenne and I would doubtless want to investigate supernatural doings in the future, now was out of the question. We had just married, just moved into a new house. We needed this time to ourselves. Billy felt that he and Solly could handle the initial tide of cases. Solly was particularly eager for the work, our initial case having kindled his appetite for something more outgoing that his boring, hermitlike retirement on the Griswold Ranch.

I did agree, if Billy thought it useful, to discuss new cases with him over the telephone once or twice a week. It had become a regular ritual. Sometimes we went out to a restaurant; sometimes Shy invited him over. But usually we spoke on the phone, and I assumed that was his agenda this morning.

I asked about the cases we had discussed last week. As we had suspected, the Spectral Shredder of Redondo Beach turned out to be a hoax, some windsurfer with phosphorescent paint and a fondness for television's *Impractical Jokers*. The haunted storeroom in the Riverside shopping mall, where noises were heard in the dead of night and objects found knocked over and rearranged in the morning, was traced to a squad of brazen rodents. The band of wailing dead migrants roaming the canyons east of San Diego, rumored to have been massacred by frustrated Border Patrol officers, proved on investigation to be a political myth spread by an Open Border organization.

"I appreciate your input on these half-assed cases, Mike, but that's not why I called. Something new has come in, and all signs point to a major investigation. I need you and Cheyenne back on the job. You've had six months for your new marriage to mature. It's time to mount up again. The Ghost Killers will have to be at full strength for this one."

"I'm not sure whether Shy would agree with

that. I don't."

"This may or may not make a difference, Mike. But the case seems almost tailor-made for you."

I felt a first tug. "Oh?"

"Yes sir," Billy continued. "It concerns a movie star. It concerns a movie star *with occult interests*."

I endured the silence until it was clear that Billy expected a response before giving out more information.

"Damn you, Billy Steele, but my fate is in your hands. I'm going to bite. Who is it?"

"Benedek Sarka. Perhaps you heard about his death? It happened a couple of weeks ago."

I knew all right, and had read some obituaries. Sarka's had been a long and distinguished career, most of it in horror films.

The genre had always intrigued me. Though the major studios of the Golden Age had tended to leave horror to Universal, most of them before their demise tried their hand on the descendants of Dracula, Frankenstein, Jekyll, The Phantom, The Mummy, The Wolf Man, She Who Must Be Obeyed, The Voodoo Queen, The Cat Woman, and all the rest. Hammer Films in England refreshed classic horror; German *krimis* pitted Scotland Yard against perverse killers in plots stemming from Edgar Wallace; Italians built up whopping body counts in their garish *gialli*. Roger Corman trained a fine generation of American directors by hiring them fresh from film schools and assigning them low-budget horror movies. In the 1980s American horror went big-time with major releases like *The Shining*, *Poltergeist*, and *Aliens*, yet left plenty of opportunity for unknown producers with embarrassing budgets and no-name casts and crews to ring the bell both financially and artistically.

No genre is more worried over, pontificated about. No genre has been better studied. A giant library records the lives of the writers, stars, makeup men, special effect artists, directors, and producers of horror movies. The books bristle with fascinating detail. Another giant library discusses the evolution of horror's subgenres, and carries on a responsible conversation about the meaning of it all. And no genre but horror has fans of sufficient dedication to support lavish restorations of every one of its landmark movies. Horror fans demand, and get, the best scholarship and the best technology.

On the day before Benedek Sarka died, you could have said that the career of no other living actor intersected more important horror films than his. In that final phase of that career, Sarka had left cinema altogether, returning to live audiences in legitimate theaters. As the manager of his own repertory company, his passion was not the usual one for Shakespeare, but was instead an intensely loyal devotion to Shakespeare's contemporary, Christopher Marlowe.

I was interested, all right. Billy had mentioned Sarka's *occult interests*. Those had not been featured in the newspaper obituaries I had seen so far. I was dying to find out what those strange fascinations were.

Feeling like a goner, I sighed theatrically and asked, "What's the job?"

Ghost Killers had been engaged by Wagner Summers, the attorney representing Robert Sarka, son and presumed heir of Benedek Sarka. Mr. Sarka's will was to be read next Tuesday at his home in Ventura. He and his son Robby were not exactly estranged, since they had apparently never been close to begin with. Through the years Benedek had let Robby know that his inheritance would include certain occult items of exceeding rarity and power. It was repeatedly impressed upon the son that he must, when the time came, be prepared to deal with these items in a proper and responsible manner. Robert Sarka, however, was not a mage. He knew little about the occult and cared less. A safe reception of the mysterious heirlooms, whatever they turned out to be, would become the job of the Ghost Killers. Mr. Summers was hiring us in Robert's name to ensure that his supernatural inheritance was passed on with all due caution.

"So. Tuesday—in Ventura, I imagine?" I remembered what my father always said about Ventura. It came back with a twinge of uneasiness.

"I thought we could all drive down together on Monday. Robby will also be inheriting, along with the hocus-pocus pieces, his father's seashore mansion just south of downtown. There's a guest house with two bedrooms, ocean views, and a fully equipped kitchen, and we've been offered its use."

"Gratis?"

"Gratis."

"Have you discussed fees?"

"It's a sizeable estate. We'll get 200K if we can actually disarm whatever may be dangerous about the occult items. If we cannot defuse the danger, or if there is no danger to begin with, then we get 25K for our trouble."

"In other words, we've arrived."

"Yeah. I guess we have at that."

"Maybe it's due to our books."

"I thought the same thing, Mike."

Later I told Cheyenne about our new commission. She smiled, brushed back some strands of lustrous brown hair, and reveled in the good news.

Eyes brightening, Shy pointed out that we had always planned to return to the Ghost Killers. Moreover, the timing couldn't be better. Instead of moving to a utilitarian rental, we would be living in what sounded like spectacular quarters, with our own kitchen and ocean view. True, we would have to share those with Billy and Solly. But they had been neighbors of hers for years now, and it would be nice to have them nearby again. If we went as planned to New Aarhus, our time would be spent supervising the workers, remaking old decisions, planning last-minute refinements. Ben knew in general what our wishes were. He could do the supervising, and address the on-the-spot issues sure to arise. The responsibility would do him good. Meantime, we would be engaged in a new case promising all sorts of secrets to fathom and mysteries to unravel.

"And dangers to face. Don't forget those."

"Not on your life, dear. Too many of those, and we'll be heading home."

I was going to tell her that this trip home was not likely to happen, since we were not the sort of people who began something and then backed off from finishing it. But at that moment my internal engine threw a belt or slipped a gear. I found myself thinking about our marriage. Maybe . . . maybe my nerves were somehow to blame for the way Cheyenne's flexibility and immense good will left me—there was no way around it—anxious, somehow unsatisfied. I wasn't sure.

Could a marriage be too perfect? Falsely perfect? There had to be something in our way. Everyone said so. We would one day encounter differences that had no Pollyanna upsides. They would have no easy fixes, and possibly no hard fixes either. They might be completely unfixable. Could we live with those kinds of differences?

Suddenly I was convinced against all reason and all evidence that I was missing something. I wanted something I was not getting. I had been telling myself over and over that my new marriage was mysteriously blissful. But in the depths of my soul another calculation was being made. That was why I kept expecting my happiness to hit a snag. I knew unconsciously that we were vulnerable. But what was it? What did I lack or we lack?

CHAPTER TWO

Come Monday morning Billy showed up wearing one of the nicest pieces from his enviable collection of vintage military clothing. It was an A-2 horsehide flight jacket, dyed a beautiful mahogany color, with soft knitted cuffs in a contrasting tan. The garment had been manufactured by Buzz Rickson's, a Japanese company devoted to making fanatically detailed reproductions of American military dress, correct in every particular, to the point of using fabrics woven on vintage looms and sewing the garments together on vintage machines. Billy told me once that he had learned about the company from a William Gibson novel.

Two generations of pilots stood behind Billy Steele. The jacket seemed to know that the right man had it on, and hung itself in flattering angles, had a way of capturing light and shadow in pleasing configurations. I knew it wouldn't look that good on me. But I loved the jacket. I've had more than one dream of swiping choice items from Billy Steele's closet.

But Cheyenne and I didn't spend long ogling our partner's dress. The main showpiece that morning was brand-new wheels. *Huge* brand-new wheels! Billy had pulled up in a Black Chrome edition 2009 Hummer H-2 with a 6.2 liter 393-hp

V8. That in itself would have been a rare car, but Billy's Hummer sported a gorgeous body color, a reddish orange from the Western sunset palette, continued in the interior leather of the front bucket seats and the captain's chairs of the second row, set against charcoal doors, floors, ceiling, and dash.

"The Sedona Metallic color," he explained proudly, "was announced as an option for the Black Chrome edition, but in the end never got released to the public. This vehicle here was owned until recently by General Motors itself."

"I really love the color," Shy said, in the low breathy tone that always meant excitement.

"It looks comfortable too," I said. "I've heard that the original Humvee-modeled Hummers had low ceilings and not much leg room."

Billy nodded. "You still might wish for a couple more inches of head room, but this version solved all of the other cabin comfort issues."

"What shall we call it?" Shy asked.

Solly Barlow walked around from the passenger side. Due in part to his new duties as proprietor of the Griswold Ranch in Black Ash Canyon, he seemed to be enjoying a personal renaissance these days. It was still wise to avoid political topics, which put conversational partners in danger of detonating one of the landmines of right-wing indignation ringing the social boundary of Barlow's ego. But the man looked happier. He seemed to have lost a few pounds, and had begun neatening his formerly unkempt beard. "I know what I call it," he announced, "a goddamn folly, that's what. Lincoln Navigator and Mercedes GL have better power, comfort, and fuel efficiency."

"But not anywhere near the strength," Billy shot back. "This is the best off-road performer ever built."

The old Solly would have clammed up at this point, keeping his disapproval of the vehicle to himself. This new Solly snorted and held his ground. "It's seven feet wide, and no good at all on a narrow trail."

"It never gets stuck, either. Try taking a Lincoln or a Benz across a stream two-feet deep or over a 12-inch boulder!"

"And how often do you do *that* in a car? On such terrain you'd be better off on horseback."

Solly would have to get used to the fact that the Hummer was here to stay. I turned to Billy. "Is this a company car?"

He nodded. "I'm entering him as a business expense."

Him, was it? Cars, like ships, were always feminine. Billy had given this guy a special honor indeed. "Well, then," I continued, "Shy is right.

We'll have to name the beast. It will give us something to do." We loaded our gear into the enormous rear compartment, and began work on the
naming chore as soon as we hit the road.

"How about the Crank Tank?" Solly muttered.
Among our better alternatives were Galloping
Ghost, SUV (Spirit Utility Vehicle), Speed Demon,
Shade Raid, Spook Magnet, Killers' Kar, War
Wagon, Hell on Wheels, and (in view of its engine
noise) Scream Queen. The flaws of the major
contenders were pointed out. Scream Queen was
feminine, Hell on Wheels was a bad Paul McCart-
ney song, Speed Demon didn't pinpoint the vehicle's distinctive attribute, etc. By the time we
caught the 101 in Lassiter Springs we had our
name, courtesy of a last-minute Billy Steele suggestion. We were traveling in the Creep Jeep.

On the highway heading south, Billy entertained
us with stories about Ventura ghost-hunting. It
was an old settlement, he reminded us, the last of
the California missions founded by Father Juni-
pero Serra himself. Such towns always had a deep
deposit of ghost lore. In Ventura's history there
were Chumash, Spanish, and Mexican ghost sightings. Most of the older buildings in town (and
there were a number of them) had been associated
with hauntings.

Ventura's ghosts were the typical ones—a

wronged Indian maid who lingered near the old mission, a woman in white who walked the upper floor of a mansion on Poli Street, a woman in black down the block, a few phantom ships in the harbor, a restless spirit or two in a downtown theater, and at least a specter each in the vintage inns and hotels. But certain decisions made by Ventura's city fathers had no doubt worsened the area's supernatural history. For example, like every modern California city to begin life as a small frontier settlement, Ventura had to face at some point the problem of its dead. The old pioneer towns kept their dead nearby, in plots usually located alongside its first churches.

But fashions changed. The deep metaphysics of a populace changed. Invariably it came to pass that a twentieth-century generation would feel their dead ought to be, not in close view, but out of sight. By 1941, following this pattern, Ventura believed that its dignity required a handsome downtown park. But what could be done about the city cemetery, which was of course smack dab in the middle of the area designated for the new park? The city forbade any further burials, forcing future customers to rest in the soil of the new Ivy Lawn Cemetery outside the city limits. Then they planted a hedge around the old graveyard and built Plaza Park around the hedge.

This arrangement sufficed until the 1960s. By then the dead needed to be further out of sight. Rethinking the downtown park in a ham-fisted manner, the city moved all the graves (or so they said) out to Ivy Lawn and dumped all the funky headstones and monuments in a big pile in Hall Canyon. For a time pranksters made sure that they migrated all over town. Supernaturally, of course, the result was a marked increase in the number of unquiet spirits beheld in Plaza Park.

Shy and I were sitting in the captain's chairs in the back seat, a divider between us the size of a large drinks tray. As Billy finished his tale of Ventura's Plaza Park blunders, I decided to break in. I had a story I was dying to tell, and this was the perfect place for it.

"You know, my father had this thing about Ventura as a cursed city. Every time a news item took place there—an accident, a crime, a mishap of some sort—my father would say, 'Well, *Ventura*—I mean, what do you expect in a city that was originally named *San Buenaventura*, "City of Good Luck," and then allowed its name to be shortened to *Ventura*, plain old "Luck," luck of any kind, good or bad, like you find in a casino? Talk about asking for it! Talk about tempting Fate! You're named "Good Fortune" and you change it to "Fortune." Like I say, what do you expect?!' Dad might have picked this up from his father. I think I remember Wilbur saying the same thing over breakfast one morning when he was reading a newspaper story about a shipwreck in Ventura Harbor."

I felt a gentle stir in the back of my mind, and knew from experience that this mental flicker was Wilbur's way of nodding yes.

"I suppose 'San Buenaventura' sounded too foreign or too Catholic," Shy offered. "Father Serra must have had St. Bonaventure in mind, the medieval theologian?"

"I believe," Billy said, "that so far as the State of California is concerned, the city is *still* San Buenaventura. They changed to the shorter colloquial form 'Ventura' on road signs, maps, and postage to avoid confusion. Their mail used to get mixed up with San Francisco and San Diego. Also, the Southern Pacific Railroad found it easier to sell tickets to 'Ventura' than to some town with a long Spanish name that half its customers and employees couldn't pronounce."

I laughed. "Typical Ventura, according to my Dad. In trying to avoid confusion they wound up creating more of it."

Billy resumed his account of Ventura's record as a haunted town.

The best-known living ghost hunter in the area

was a failed Chevy dealer named Roger Drivell, who had managed to parlay his supernatural hobbies into a thriving business organizing and leading ghost tours around the world. His leisure-ly, low-key books (*Ventura Ghosts*, *Hollywood Ghosts*, *San Francisco Ghosts*, etc.) had established him as an authority on the California supernatural. Drivell was the go-to guy on this particular sub-ject. If a Los Angeles TV station wanted to mount a program on the ten Halloween séances held at the Knickerbocker Hotel in the hope that Houdi-ni's spirit could leave a message for his widow in their prearranged secret code, Drivell would be the most prominent guest, charged with narrating the crucial anecdotes. Whenever a local story with occult overtones broke, Drivell would be the main interview for print and media journalists. An old hand at this game, he knew how to whip up public interest without really saying anything.

Drivell never disturbed with dire predictions or alarming analogues to controversial events. He would tell a personal story or two, perhaps con-cerning the time his team of investigators had looked into a supposed haunting at the same location where a spirit happening had recently been observed. His wife Nellie, a medium, had known immediately that negative energy, disap-pointed female negative energy, seethed in the building. When asked if he believed that a ghost had really been seen last week, he would milk a smile for all it was worth, giving the impression that he knew far more than he was willing to say. "Of course I don't really know," he would reply. "But on the other hand, I couldn't rule out the possibility."

"In other words," Billy declared, "Drivell doesn't know a thing, but has made it appear as if that hotel is being haunted by an angry female ghost. Before long, if the hotel is still in business, he'll be taking twenty people there on Roger Drivell's Haunted Los Angeles guided tour. The man's an embarrassment to the profession."

Shy wanted some more examples of Drivell's lame reasoning, and Billy was eager to supply them. "I've been reading his book on *Haunted Ventura* as preparation for our trip, so I'm well stocked with instances of the Drivell mind at work. In one chapter he writes about the haunting of a local adobe that once housed a prominent Mexican family, but is now a protected historical attraction. Drivell instructed his team to wander around and stop wherever they "felt" some spectral presence. Lo and behold, many of them marked exactly the same places where ghosts had been seen! However, the adobe only had three or four rooms in it, and ghosts had been reported in all of its rooms. It would have been impossible for the team *not* to find ghost hot spots! This is typical Drivell—to act as if something remarkable occurred when it was just more of the ordinary."

On another foray Drivell asked his team to draw pictures of ghosts, since the "artistic self" and the "psychic self" reside in the same area of the brain. Billy was withering on this trashy piece of wisdom. "Is art so simple that its creation uses only one sector of the brain? Also, I am not aware of any research seeking to trace a 'psychic self' to a particular brain locale. It would be a tough scientific project to pursue, since you would first have to establish that there is such a thing as a 'psychic self,' which I strongly doubt. I wonder. . . . Do we know which sector of the brain lying or idiocy occur in? All of them, I would think."

"Very funny," Shy admitted. "I can see we are dealing with a fool. But is he always so benighted? Does he never say anything . . . I don't know . . . *interesting*?"

Billy surprised me by nodding agreement. "Actually, yes. One of the chapters deals with a Rudolph Valentino sighting. As you may know, Valentino is the top Hollywood ghost in terms of number of appearances and number of sites appeared at. Far more than John Barrymore or Marilyn Monroe or James Dean, Elvis, Lennon, Michael

Jackson, whomever. There must be twenty different spots in Los Angeles that claim Valentino
sightings. There's a hotel in Santa Maria where
Rudy haunts Room 221, in which he supposedly
stayed for a night back in the days when Santa
Maria was Central City. Anyway, Drivell has a
chapter on a Valentino sighting near Ventura, in
the town of Oxnard, just a few miles south. It
begins with a welcome spell of historical reasoning. The Valentino ghost was seen in a beach
house he purportedly rented while filming *Son of
the Sheik* in 1926. However, that movie was not
even filmed in Oxnard. *The Sheik* was in 1921,
when the sand dunes of old Oxnard stood in for
the Sahara Desert. Drivell establishes that Valentino in 1921 had indeed rented a home in the area.
So a haunting was at least technically possible. He
doesn't mention that, if Valentino haunted all the
places he resided, he would the busiest globetrot-
ter in spirit history, dividing his time between
Italy, New York, and California.

"But at the end of the Valentino discussion it
enters Drivell's head that many of the ghosts he
discusses in his book were famous in life. Why is
this? Why do the famous seem to return from
death in such inordinate numbers?"

I checked the reactions of my fellow passengers.
Both Solly and Shy looked lost in thought. It was

certainly true that many of the world's most famous ghosts had been famous as living human beings. Great Caesar's Ghost and the like.

Billy put our thoughts in order.

"Maybe they *don't* return. Most ghost reports are either made up or imagined. People see what they want to see. They want to catch a glimpse of the famous, the same in death as they did in life. But Drivell speculates that famous people *do* return as ghosts in greater numbers than ordinary joes and janes. The famous usually desire fame. They always had the urge that others be aware of them, that they be seen and known, and this carries over into death."

Silence fell on the Creep Jeep. "Yes," I finally said. "That theory would explain a lot, if one assumed that ghost reports were largely accurate. There's a class of ghost that lusts for fame, and comes back from the grave to press itself yet again on living consciousness."

We batted the idea around for a while. Drivell's theory did not fit the ghosts we had battled in the Black Ash Canyon Case. Fame-yearning was certainly not the most common motive behind a haunting. That would be, we were agreed, revenge in its many guises. But it was a possibility worth bearing in mind that there might be a class of fame-crazed spirits, desperate to clear places for themselves in living minds.

I removed some pages from my briefcase. "Listen, I did some research over the weekend on this Benedek Sarka, whose estate we're supposed to secure or de-haunt or whatever the job turns out to be. One piece that turned up was especially useful. It's called "The Startling Career of Benedek Sarka," and was published three years ago in a highly regarded specialist film journal called *Video Watchdog*, which bills itself as 'The perfectionist's guide to fantastic cinema.' I think the word *fantastic* there means any suspension of realism—a magic object, a magic being like a fairy godmother or a werewolf, a future setting, a setting far back enough to accommodate fantastic elements, like the Middle Ages, the classical world, prehistoric times. Anyway, this account of Sarka was written by an academic, but it's clear and informative and only a few pages long. I could read it aloud, if you want."

With the consent of the group, I began reading.

Benedek Fekete Sarka was the son of Lily Fekete Sarka, a talented painter, and Hungarian industrialist Jelek Sarka. Jelek left his native Hungary in the political turmoil following World War I, relocating in Manchester, England. It was there that Sarka Locks, heretofore a small manufacturer of a line of padlocks employing around thirty people, began to expand and diversify, acquiring the new name of Sarka Steel International. Jelek built a many-tentacled global corporation marketing luggage, safes, gun cases, strong boxes, bank vaults, shipping compartments, and prison cells, besides handcuffs and other locking restraints used in law enforcement and mental health facilities. Their only child Benedek was born in 1929. In 1935, again troubled by the future of Europe, Jelek brought his company to America, settling in the small coastal town of Ventura, California.

Lily Sarka had from childhood been fascinated by ghosts and fairies, omens and portents. As an artist she gravitated toward Mondrian, with his theosophical interests, and Delaunay, with his adaptation of Hermetic motifs. In California, however, her artistic output declined, and she fell into a depression from which she never recovered. In November 1939 she drowned in the treacherous tides of "Folly's Cove," as the waters bordering on the Sarka estate are aptly named.

In an especially varied career, Benedek Sarka left his mark on numerous facets of the motion picture business. He was first of all interested in establishing a division of Sarka Steel to manufacture motion picture equipment, cameras and lighting gear primarily. Benedek thought it feasible to replace with an acetate base the standard nitrate film in use throughout the industry, despite its well-known drawbacks of flammability and gradual chemical deterioration. He experimented with lighter and more precise mechanisms for controlling the speed at which film moved through a camera, and developed the rudiments of a new process for transferring 16mm film, generally associated with home movies, onto theatre-ready 35mm stock.

These technical interests descended to Benedek from his father. The maternal side of the young man was fascinated with occultism and the arts, and his dedication to these pursuits seems to have escalated with his mother's death. Benedek designed various 16mm cameras, and had them built in the nearby San Diego factory of Sarka Steel. He used some of these prototypes to shoot experimental films starring himself and his acquaintances in Los Angeles, where he eventually attended the film program at Occidental College. His works from this period include *Là-Bas* (*The Damned*), a twenty-minute collage of various linked sensations based in a general way on the infamous occult novel by Joris-Karl Huysmans; *Shroud Bound*, a short fantasia inspired by the enigmatic last paragraphs of Poe's *The Narrative of Arthur Gordon Pym*, where a shrouded white figure at the entrance to the South Pole claims the life of Pym's one remaining traveling companion; and *Seventh Degree*, a film that has not been screened for decades, and may no longer exist, but was said by one viewer, underground director Stan Brakhage, who watched this elusive private movie in 1951 at the home of Sarka himself, to anticipate the magical rituals later filmed by his erstwhile friend Kenneth Anger (*Inauguration of the Pleasure Dome* [1954-1966]; *Invocation of My Demon Brother* [1969]; *Lucifer Rising* [1970-1981]).

Many film actors go behind the camera after a career in front of it. But Sarka, ever the nonconformist, graduated from an early directorial period to film acting. After small roles in *Nightmare Alley* (1947) and *The Ghost of Rashmon Hall* (1948), he played one of Vincent Price's more memorable victims in *House of Wax* (1953). Then Sarka surfaced in Europe as, among others, a mesmerized servant in Hammer's *Horror of Dracula* (1958); a baffled policeman in Mario Bava's *The Girl Who Knew Too Much* (AKA *The Evil Eye*, 1963); an interested spectator in Jess Franco's *Venus in Furs* (1969) and a rival vampire hunter in the same director's *Vampyros Lesbos*

(1971); a smitten caretaker in Luciano Ercoli's *Death Walks on High Heels* (1971); the town vendor in Sergio Martino's *Torso* (1973); and finally as an enigmatic blind man in Dario Argento's *Suspiria* (1975). It was during these years in Italy, the classic period of the *giallo*, that Sarka met and married Allegra Malatesti, daughter of Cesar Malatesti, head of Casa Editrice Malatesti, a centuries-old publishing house in Florence. The firm would eventually issue Sarka's esoteric study of Christopher Marlowe (*The Horror of the Conquered* [2001]).

His new bride in tow, the actor returned to America. Jelek had died in 1975, during the filming of *Suspiria*, leaving Benedek virtually his entire fortune, including the beachfront mansion just south of Ventura. Allegra gave birth to a boy, Robert Sarka, in Ventura in 1976. Benedek must have appreciated the irony: just after inherited wealth had freed him from the rat race, his acting career zoomed to new heights of popularity. He was the resourceful Magus of *Razor Sharp* (1978), a Van Helsing-like Robert Shaw figure in the immensely successful *Vampire Sharks* (1979), and a frighteningly helpful clerk in *Halloween Costume Sale* (1980), another blockbuster that spawned numerous sequels.

But Sarka refused to appear in them. Allegra, swimming one morning in 1982 at Folly's Cove, was swept out to sea by the powerful riptide. Her death was ruled an accident, but there were rumors at the time that Allegra Sarka was, like Benedek's mother before her, her own victim. Soon thereafter, in 1983, Benedek declared that he was bored with horror films, bored with cinema itself. He was preparing a major career change, moving away from cinema altogether to explore its ancient roots in live theatre. He gave interviews about the cheap sensationalism of modern horror films, their willingness to shock us with attacks on the body rather than with ideas. For a fuller experience of horror, Benedek maintained, one must return to Marlowe and Seneca.

Sarka was not the first actor in horror films whose abiding dream was to retrieve the working world of the nineteenth-century actor/manager, and take his place alongside Henry Irving, Edwin Booth, and Johnston Forbes-Robinson. John Carradine tried to achieve this transition in the early 1940s. While filming poverty-row shockers like *Voodoo Man* and *Return of the Ape Man* by day, he performed Shakespeare plays by night in Pasadena and San Francisco. The hope was to found a repertory company to be known as "John Carradine and His Shake-spearean Players." A mini-tour featuring, on successive nights, *The Merchant of Venice*, *Othello*, and *Hamlet*, played two-week engagements in San Francisco, Seattle, Portland, and finally at the Biltmore Theatre in Los Angeles. There the venture folded in the face of booking apathy.

At the height of this ambition, Carradine had purchased the Elsinore stage set from John Bar-rymore's 1922 Broadway *Hamlet*, which had been designed by the legendary Roger Edmond Jones. This set, he hoped, would one day grace his own triumphant version of the Prince of Denmark. It was also a deeply satisfying idea to link his stage career to that of John Barrymore, his personal idol and former drinking compan-ion. Had not the Great Profile himself played a large role in the first wave of Hollywood horror through his performances in *The Sea Beast*, *Dr. Jekyll and Mr. Hyde*, *Svengali*, and *The Mad Geni-us*?

But unlike John Carradine, Benedek Sarka had at his disposal a considerable fortune. He was indeed able to finance a touring company, The Deptford Players, given over to the dramatic works of Christopher Marlowe with Sarka him-self planted in the leading roles. Admittedly, *Dido, Queen of Carthage* and *The Massacre at Paris* were not performed so often as *Tamburlaine the Great*, Parts I and II, *Edward the Second*, *The Jew of Malta*, and *Doctor Faustus*, but even the two relatively neglected plays *were* performed. The enterprise was surprisingly successful at attracting a younger audience to suburban auditoriums, converted movie palaces, and dinner theatres to sit spellbound before Benedek Sarka's occult-laced productions of Marlowe's savage plays. In 2005 the company's *Doctor Faustus* and *Tamburlaine the Great* were captured by the cameras of the Public Broadcasting Service.

As to why his passion ran to Marlowe rather than Shakespeare, Sarka has a great deal to say. Much of his critical study, *The Horror of the Conquered*, is devoted to this question. He dates his Marlowe obsession from 1942, when as a young man he traveled with his father to London. While Jelek Sarka engaged in munitions negotiations with the British government, Benedek was able to see the great Peter Brook's first theatrical production. "It was *Doctor Faustus* at the ominously named Torch Theatre in London. I was enthralled."

In the last phase of his career Sarka came to believe that Marlowe, given his flagrant exploitation of sadomasochistic themes, held deeper lessons for our age than the more maudlin

Shakespeare. Marlowe's drama is founded on extremity of conquest and extremity of defeat. In those, Sarka maintains, we see the absolutes: "With that polarity revealed before us, all fates can be plotted." Fans of the horror film sometimes complain that Benedek Sarka abandoned or betrayed them. In fact, he left scary movies to sup full of a horror he considered far more profound.

"That's it," I finished. The quiet didn't last long.

"My Lord," Solly said with a partly mock shiver. "A fixation on what is more horrible, what is less, with a preference for the more. . . . He doesn't seem a warm man, does he?"

"I admit," Billy added, "that I don't relish the thought of handling his collection of occult trinkets. And you're dead right about the place name, Mike. Ventura wasn't so *buena* for the two Sarka wives who drowned just off the family beach!"

Cheyenne laughed. "I gather *Doctor Faustus* is his favorite play? I'm not sure what *that* says about the man."

"It means," I suggested, "that he was after extremity, as Peter Brook was as well in adapting Artaud's theatre of cruelty. This case could go in all sorts of odd directions." I was about to say where exactly this case could go when Billy took over. I think he knew what was on my mind, and decided the wiser course would be to leave it unsaid for now.

"I agree with that. But shall we let it all go for now, and listen to some music?" When we had given him the OK, he put in a homemade CD with some vintage electric rockers by the likes of Robert Gordon, Stone Jungle, The Blasters, and George Thorogood and the Destroyers.

An hour later we exited the 101 in downtown Ventura. It took us a while to double back and turn south, but we soon arrived at the only house overlooking Folly's Cove. Through the wrought iron fence we saw lawn, flower beds, tall shrubs, pines, and several thick palm trees.

Beyond these plantings, on the ocean side of the property, segments of a large stone building were visible. Billy pushed a button and soon the gates buzzed open.

The Creep Jeep entered the grounds. It had done its job, and the Ghost Killers were on the scene.

CHAPTER THREE

We looked around the periphery of the rectangular house before knocking on the front door. Its gray stones, probably cut from the hills to the east of town, were streaked with random patches of white. Though the white areas looked as if they might have been done in the heat of the moment by some wannabe Jackson Pollack, Billy thought these efflorescences had accrued slowly from decades of salt-heavy fogs and winds.

At the back of the house, facing the sea, was a large patio with wrought-iron tables and heavy wooden deck chairs. The modern windows on this back wall contrasted with the lines of mullioned windows on the landward side. A thick stone wall skirted the edge of the cliff on which the house had been constructed. Fifty feet below was the happy nook of Folly's Cove, guarded on both sides by points of rugged rocks. The air teemed with sound. Cawing gulls and barking pelicans brought life to the waves' relentless thud and hiss. To the south wooden stairs, painted white, led down to a sandy beach strewn with masses of kelp. Beyond the stairs was a line of high thick oleanders with a pathway through the center. It led, we supposed, to the guest quarters we were to occupy.

An oddity of the home's architecture could only be discerned from the back patio. That is, the house appeared from the front to be a two-story structure. But in the southwestern corner was a square turret rising to a third floor. This was the mansion's highest vantage and presumably its most spectacular sea view.

We were greeted at the front door by a stout woman in her fifties with graying dark hair, rouged cheeks, and a ready smile. She introduced herself as Marta Barabas, the Sarka housekeeper. Attached to the name was a joke. "Some people find that 'Marta' is too close to 'martyr.' If you are one of those, you may call me 'Marty.'" Her grandmother, as a teenage kitchen assistant, had accompanied Jelek and Lily Sarka in their move from Budapest to Manchester, then later as head chef followed the Sarkas to Ventura. Here in America she fell in love with a local restaurateur, and in the 1950's gave birth to Marta's mother Rosa. By the time Marta came along, via Rosa's marriage to a house painter, the grandmother had returned to Hungary. Rosa was the new Sarka chef and housekeeper, and at Benedek's invitation settled with her family in the guest house. Now that the couple was retired in Arizona, Marta had inherited the family sinecure. We didn't ask if she had ever married, and later learned she had not.

Our tour of her domain began with the newly modernized kitchen. Marta's smile relaxed as she joyfully praised the new French cabinets, the orange and turquoise marble counters, the rust-colored Italian tile, the six-burner gas stove, the double convection ovens, the two dishwashers, and so on. To the north of this show place was the dining room, its windows open to the front lawns and gardens. Between the two rooms was a pantry with storage chests and a large table where food could be staged before delivery to the dining room and dirty dishes stowed on their way back to the kitchen.

The cavernous living room with its beamed ceiling and parquet flooring was filled with comfortable leather chairs and couches, most of its furniture centered on the twin picture windows. A large stone fireplace gave the space another *raison d'etre*, and so did the flat television screen against the north wall. On the same wall hung a canvas signed by Lily Sarka. I saw the influence of Mondrian, mentioned in the *Video Watchdog* essay, in the blocks of red, blue, yellow, black, and white. Here the color masses together formed an image of Folly's Cove underneath a titanic vibrating sun. I liked the painting immediately.

There were two downstairs bedrooms in the north wing, one of which had been converted into an office. A conference table occupied one end of the room. "This is where Mr. Summers will read the will tomorrow afternoon at 1:00," the housekeeper informed us.

Upstairs we saw three more bedrooms and a game room. Marta herself used the smallest of these upstairs rooms. It seemed quite large to me, and was graced by a picture window view of the ever-but-never-changing sea. A door separated this area from the master suite in the southeastern corner, which could also be reached from the first floor by its own private staircase.

But much the most arresting part of the tour was on the first floor, where a roomy entranceway flowed inward from the front door. This area opened out on one side to the kitchen and dining room, and on the other to the master bedroom stairs, the entirely enclosed turret, and finally the living room. The point of interest was a large wooden door—the only entrance to the three rooms stacked on top of each other in the southwestern tower.

The turret, Marta said, had not been original to the house. Benedek had designed it and supervised the construction in 1976, soon after moving into the mansion. It was his only major modification to the Folly's Cove property. Marta—none of us felt much attraction to "Marty"—swore she had never set foot in the two upper chambers. Benedek Sarka himself had always cleaned and maintained them. The actor met her standards, given what she observed during rare audiences in the bottom floor of the new tower. That room was no more or less than Benedek Sarka's personal book-lined study. There he planned his Marlowe productions, wrote his book on the playwright, and conducted his personal correspondence. The study's wooden bookcases got occasional treatments with an old-recipe almond polish, and the floors were vacuumed, the windows washed, often enough to prevent the housekeeper from demanding full access.

Benedek had made it clear that the two higher rooms were off limits for everyone but himself. Marta was forbidden to visit them, and to make sure that her curiosity never got the best of her, the door from the main house to the tower staircase was kept double locked. Should this barrier be breached, the stairwell doors to the higher rooms were also locked. An hour after Benedek had died in the County Hospital, his personal lawyer Wagner Summers had arrived at the mansion with written instructions from Mr. Sarka that the tower be locked down until the reading of the will and passing of certain documents to Robert Sarka. Benedek had provided him with a set of keys.

The door appeared to be an ordinary yellowy brown wood finished in a clear stain. If anything hinting at oddity struck your eye, it was the unusually large T-frame steel straps attaching the door to its hinges. Marta told us that door had been fashioned from a rare Argentinian quebracho wood, the densest on earth. Its planks, heavier than water, didn't float. One of the two locks was a conventional deadbolt operated by the door knob. The other, which I believed was called a "privacy lock," was a side bolt keyed to a plate above the knob. The hardware was hammered copper. Marta, embellishing her master's eccentricity, had kept it shining. A geometrical design was etched on the knob. Beneath the keyhole one could read in raised letters "Sarka Locks," and in smaller letters underneath, "Manchester, England." Professional glances passed between the Ghost Killers. If there were spooks in Folly's Cove, we knew where they lived.

"Isn't there a tradition of putting book-filled offices in towers?" Billy asked.

I knew something about that. "Well, there's a famous tower in the Dordogne designed by Michel de Montaigne. It also had three floors. On the bottom was a chapel, on the second floor a bedroom, and on the third a large library and a study where Montaigne probably wrote his *Essays*."

Billy nodded. "But here the study and the books are on the first floor."

"That's right. And I doubt whether there is a bedroom in this tower, since the master suite is just behind it. I think the tradition, both literary and architectural, puts the study at the top of the tower. There are some lines in John Milton's *Il Penseroso* about retiring to a high lonely tower and reading all night, even summoning the ghosts of dead authors."

"I would imagine," Billy continued, "that someone designing a tower would tend to dedicate the top room to his favorite pursuit or highest ideal."

"You think so?!" Solly scoffed. "How picturesque for the scholar to gaze at a grand view when not wasting his eyeballs on some fool book. You people have your heads in the clouds. The tower? That's the best place to catch sight of your approaching enemies. If you have any brains in your head, you put your sharpest guards in the highest room."

After the tour, Marta served us coffee and rolls in her fine new kitchen. We asked her about Robert. Why wasn't he here yet? What was wrong between him and his father? What kind of man was he?

The room fell silent as the housekeeper gradually absorbed our questions. "You call yourselves

Ghost Killers, whatever that means. I have no idea what it is you actually *do*. But you seem to be decent people. Perhaps you can bring some peace to Robert. I hope so. My greatest fear is that he will sell Folly's Cove at once, possibly to a developer. Maybe you can cure his lifelong hatred for this home. For that reason, and in that hope, I will help you as best I can."

She sat down at the breakfast table, and we gathered around her. "Robby Sarka will not arrive until tomorrow afternoon. I begged him to sleep here, but he prefers a hotel in Oxnard. I'll keep working on him! Many years ago, he told me on the telephone, he vowed never to spend another night in this house. According to my mother, he and his father were at odds with each other throughout Robby's childhood. When Benedek Sarka came up in conversation, the boy would just change the subject or pretend not to have heard.

"He must have specific grudges. He probably feels in general that the house is cursed, and that his father deliberately courted disaster by continuing to live here. Our local tides took the life of his grandmother. When he was only six years old, his mother also drowned.

I interrupted her. "On several internet sites there is mention of Lily and Allegra's deaths being possible suicides. Do you know anything about that?"

"Maybe," she said, her face reddening. "Lily left a note, I believe. She had never adapted fully to England, and felt even more isolated in California. She read. She lost interest in her art. I see great joy in the painting that hangs in the living room, but it is her only major California work. Sadly, it depicts the cove where she was swept out to sea and drowned. The sudden riptides in these waters are truly dangerous! Nearby are publicly owned beaches where the State of California refuses to post lifeguards. You swim at your own risk. I advise you not to swim in Folly's Cove. We used to put NO SWIMMING signs down there, but they kept getting washed away."

We murmured our assent.

"As to Allegra's death. . . . Benny told me around a decade ago that she had been unfaithful to him. Repeatedly unfaithful. The worst of her escapades was an affair with a rich furrier who sailed by our cove one afternoon and saw Allegra sunbathing. He dared her to swim out to his yacht for a cocktail. She did it. One thing led to another, one afternoon to many afternoons. I remember my mother telling me, as a lesson in caution, that Allegra loved a dare and could never refuse one. Unlike Lily, she left no suicide note. But I believe, since my source is once again my mother, that Allegra had a long and disturbing talk with Robby on the day before she died.

"Her death changed Benedek. He decided to spend the balance of his career performing before live audiences. That meant traveling most of the time. He hired a governess to supervise the boy, and he wanted to hire a personal tutor as well, so that his son could be spared the crudities and indignities of public school. But Robby carried on against the tutor idea so stubbornly that he was finally sent, as he wished to be, to the Ventura public school system.

"Once Robby got a foothold in the world beyond this house, he never looked back. Benedek expected him to relish art or literature. Robby was instead taken with mathematics and engineering. Benedek implored him to help himself to the family fortune for any purpose whatsoever. Robby refused to touch it. His father expected, at a minimum, ordinary civility. But Robert in his adulthood has refused to visit this place even for a meal that would last no more than an hour. The truth is, Robby Sarka has not spent a second in this house since the day of his high school graduation in 1994."

She paused, looking us over, then broke out in a smile. "But enough of old wounds and sorrows. Let me show you the guest house."

She marched us out the front door and onto the path leading through the oleander hedge. We found ourselves in a pocket universe. The property was smaller. I estimated that it was about a quarter the size of the grounds we had just left. But it was just as private, surrounded by mature trees. "Look there!" Billy exclaimed, pointing to a corner of the lot. "We have our own driveway."

The one-story cottage, rimmed with flower beds, had probably been built of redwood. At least the building was stained a redwood color. In the front of the house was a kitchen and dining room on one side, a living room with a big fireplace on the other. In the back was a hallway joining two bedrooms, each with its own full bath. Outside, between the cottage and the cliff edge, was a comfortable deck reachable by doorway from both bedrooms.

"I could provide you with a cold supper tonight. We shall see how things go tomorrow. Perhaps I will do a meal for all my visitors tomorrow night. After that, I'm afraid, you're on your own. There are two fine supermarkets on California Boulevard."

"We brought our own food, but thank you for the invitation," Shy said. "We'll be fine tonight. Do you have to clean both of these houses, Marta? There seems to be an awful lot of work here."

"A local Mexican girl named Alma, a very good worker, helps me twice a week with the heavy cleaning. When it comes to the cooking in my house, I manage it entirely by myself, like my mother before me. She was a fine old-fashioned chef. It tickles me to remember the cream, the butter, the sauces." She swept us all with a naughty eye. "I don't want to boast of my talents, but I think of myself as a fine modern chef. As you will see, I have not abandoned altogether the cream, the butter, or the *sauces fines*." We got another leisurely scan, this time with a cocked eyebrow above her sparkling eye. All of us were nodding. "Excellent," Cheyenne chanted. "Hallelujah!" Solly roared.

Marta showed us the cabinets in the kitchen, which were stocked with dishes and cooking gear. If we preferred to cook outdoors, there was a grill on the patio. She led us with evident pride to the computer jack in the living room. Then, with a warm farewell, she walked off and let us be. Billy followed so that he could move the Creep Jeep down the street to our new address.

He soon returned, hauling two coolers of food into the kitchen. Solly and Shy brought in our suitcases and disappeared into the back bedrooms. Billy gestured for me to join him in the kitchen as he arranged our food in the refrigerator.

"Did you notice the design on the doorknob of the turret entrance?"

"Not really. I noticed that there *was* a design."

"A pentacle, the universal sign of magic for binding what you conjure. It's clear to me that Benedek was a dabbler in the black arts. This case may involve a ghost or two, but everything about it stinks of dark-side magic."

I nodded. "His favorite play is the classic staging of the Faust myth. Black magic is used to call forth the spirit of Helen of Troy. There's something odd about his focus on Marlowe."

"If you get a chance, Mike, do more internet research on Sarka and black magic. In the meantime, let's not bother Shy and Solly with our speculations. We'll know a lot more tomorrow when the will is read and that turret unlocked."

I agreed with the temporary secrecy. Until we had concrete information, it was best not to discuss these matters with Cheyenne. Black magic, which I knew to be symbiotic with standard religion, could bring to the fore potential conflicts in our outlooks.

Billy seemed to have dinner well in hand. Shy suggested that we go down to the beach. I put on my trunks. Though we had vowed not to swim, nothing had been said about wading. Shy wore a kind of reverse mermaid outfit: a sweatshirt up above, bikini bottoms below. It had the effect of focusing my thought beams on the below half.

We passed through the Oleander barrier, leaving our beautiful little pocket universe, and went down the white stairs to the beach. We sat on the sand for a while, gazing out at the three crags of Anacapa Island thirty miles away. It was a clear day. On the distant horizon line I thought I might be seeing the ghostly light blue mass of distant Santa Nicholas Island.

Shy arose to announce her interest in exploring the rocks at the southern end of the cove. I stayed put, and began to organize my next computer research session. That article in *Video Watchdog* seemed to know more than it actually put into words. Maybe I could look up the author? I had already done some research on the traditions of western magic, enough to know that one often found discussions of "magick," with a "k" at the end. What did that mean? This was a vast subject. I tried to come up with a list of precise internet search tags. *Christopher Marlowe and black magic.* That one needed work. *Christopher Marlowe and black magic* would turn up a welter of academic literary criticism. *Magic and magick. Film and black magic. Sex and black magick.* Those would all be revealing.

"Mike!" Shy was waving at me from the southern tip of the cove. "Come on over here! I've found something."

When I got to her, she reached out and clasped my hand. "There's a cave here. You won't believe what's in it."

She led me through a slant opening into a small cavern, maybe ten feet in length, with a sandy bottom. A shaft of afternoon sunlight pierced the entrance, enough for us to see the remains of two rock paintings. The first seemed to be an abstract occult diagram. The overall pattern was a nest of white concentric circles. On their widening edges were groups of red and orange triangular arrowheads, their tips pointing outwards in the four cardinal directions. I had a vague idea of what this was. Years back at the University of Virginia I had taken a Senior Seminar in "Occultism from the Renaissance to the Present Day." The diagram was a variety of *yantra*, a mystical picture, as opposed to a *mantra*, a mystical saying or proverb. Most yantras had to do with the flow of energy.

The next rock held images of human beings. Sections of the painting had washed away. It seemed to be a side view of three figures. One was a man wearing some sort of priestly vestment, an embroidered hat with a little curtain in back. He rested on his hands and knees. Another man in a mask with animal features took him from behind. A woman lay prone beneath the priest. She licked the bottom of his cock. On her stomach was a large but shallow bowl, into which his ejaculate fell in a line of cartoon chevrons. I thought about the first image. In the sex rites of the three figures one beheld an incarnate version of those arrowheads of fiery energy shooting to the periphery of expanding circles. Energy flowed from the cock of the man doing anal intercourse, from the red triangular tongue of the woman licking, and from the licked cock at the center of the image ejaculating into the wide mouth of the bowl. There the distillate of this magical power flow came to rest.

The lid was off our case now. This picture left no doubt about the dark insides of Sarka's legacy. I freely shared my thoughts with Shy.

"You believe that somebody, probably Benedek Sarka, had sex in this cave in order to secure a magic reward?"

"Yes. Even the setting fits—the push-pull, in-out of tides. These pictures represent or commemorate some variety of Eastern sex magic. The goal is almost always a cosmic expansion of consciousness, using sex to transcend sex. The ejaculating man is having a vision."

Shy thought for a moment. "You know, Mike, I wonder what my mother would make of this."

That surprised me. "Why?"

"Experience. I think she's had some form of sexual communication with ghosts."

"With Herrera?"

"Almost certainly. The way she spoke of him, 'my angel,' 'my silver king.' I think he possessed her in every way he could."

I wondered why she had chosen this moment to broach such an astounding deduction.

Billy's burgers were topnotch. "Nothing melts like American," he declared, finishing the grilling with thick slices of processed cheese. Our sides were baked beans and a generous bowl of his German grandmother's potato salad. After dinner the Ghost Killers drank cold beer and chatted before a glorious California sunset.

I excused myself and went inside, plugging my laptop into the living room jack. After reading about sexual magic for an hour, I reached a fuller understanding of the cave paintings. This variety of sexual magic stemmed from the Vamamarga or "Left Hand Path" of Tantras, an early, explicitly sexual form of Buddhist and Hindu ritual meditation centering on orgasm. These rites were unusual in including women. The Sanskrit word *Vama* meant "woman" as well as "left."

I kept reading, making headway in related areas. I acquired a broad sense of who mattered in the western tradition of black magic. For importing Tantric sex magic to the West, the main early figures were the American spiritualist Paschal Beverly Randolph and Madame Helena Blavatsky. The fusion of eastern sex magic and western black magic became complete in the works of the prolific British magus Aleister Crowley. (He was the wordsmith who hitched a pseudo-archaic "k" to the word "magic" in order to distinguish mage magick from stage magic.)

I also stumbled across some information that might account for the copper knob and lock plates on the turret door. Copper was used in magic to return a negative spell onto the person who sent it originally. That door was guarded against aggressive magic as well as muscles and tools.

Working outward from the piece in *Video Watchdog*, I read material related to the modern history of black magic in Southern California. I followed the restless career of the Satan-worshipping rocket scientist Jack Parsons, including the delicious tale of how he was scammed by the young L. Ron Hubbard, later the founder of Dianetics and Scientology. Parsons, like most of the key figures in Southern California black magic, belonged to the Agape Lodge of the Ordo Templi Orientis (OTO) in Pasadena. The OTO was a magical order of German origin that by 1912 was deeply under the sway of Aleister Crowley. Though the sorcerer lived for a time in America and passed through Hollywood, his directives came primarily from Europe.

It amused me to compare Crowley's OTO with Hubbard's Scientology. Like all the old magical orders, the OTO experienced chronic shortages in its operating funds. Dues were paid by members in the hope that the cult's leaders would eventually allow them access to higher planes of occult knowledge, most of which had to do with angels and demons. In Scientology, this older fund of esoteric knowledge mutated into science fiction. Aliens replaced angels and demons. Advanced civilizations from distant galaxies, not the inhabitants of Heaven and Hell, were secretly directing the course of human history.

Along with that change, Hubbard did not wait until his members seemed "ready" for high-level initiation. Truth had a fixed price. The upper layers of esoteric revelation were open to any scientologist who paid it. Hubbard's mystical lodge had rarely been in need of funds. Why? Mr.

Wonderful on TV's *Shark Tank* could tell you straight off. It had a superior business model. Tax-free religion status didn't hurt either. "If you want to get rich," Hubbard remarked, "start a religion."

When I returned to our bedroom, the deck was deserted and Shy already asleep. Before long I was too.

I woke with a jolt from feverish dreams. My nerve-ends stung with brightness, as if I had just chugged a foaming shake of electrolytes. I had a raging hard-on. Waking up with one of those was not all that unusual of course, but my mind was revving like a Grand Prix leader. In less than a minute I scanned over concrete images of a hundred or so ways that my wife and I could masturbate each other in order to prolong, segment, and sculpt our orgasms, especially mine. The next minute I scanned a hundred more ways. My mind was like a molten cauldron with a cold computer chip at its center. I had the ability to imagine large sets of permutations with dizzying exactitude. My heart raced. I was horny as a stag, horny as the devil. Those cave paintings seemed to have left a deep and potent impression.

I threw water on my face in the bathroom and plugged my sexual geysers with stones of will.

Then I slipped through the curtain, opened the sliding door, and walked out on the back deck.

"Couldn't sleep, Mike?" It was Billy Steele's voice. I could make out his form in one of the lounges. I slipped onto a neighboring one.

"Nasty dreams. Any beer left?"

I heard a cap pop. He handed me a cold bottle of Lone Star. Billy kept probing until he knew something about my nasty dreams.

"So. Shy was masturbating you, teaching you to slow down and retard your orgasm? I'm not sure what this means, if anything. But I had similar dreams."

"Really?" Billy hadn't seen the cave paintings, had not even been told about them, unless Shy had brought him up to speed while I was working at the computer. I quickly ascertained that he *didn't* know about them. So I told him what we had found down at the beach. "I assumed that those paintings had inspired my dreams, but that theory is out the window now. Were your dreams exactly like mine?"

"Just about. At first my partner was Marta Barabas. Then. . . . I hope this won't irritate you." He laughed. "Then my partner was Shy."

That laugh of his, turning his dreams into an amusing joke between beer drinkers, made it worse. I knew that Billy and Shy had grown up on adjacent ranches, and had for some years been inseparable playmates. For a time they were probably in love with each other, as childhood friends living in the same neighborhood often are.

Shy still enjoyed his company. She always seemed a little brighter and happier when Billy was around. My brain boiled and spat. I felt that our leader's self-control, usually so solid and unquestionable, had fallen down on the job. Was Billy Steele destined to be the villain of my second marriage? I was furious with him.

I asked him gruffly if he had another beer. He handed me a second Lone Star.

"Look," Billy began. "Our dreams could come from shared memories. Did you watch Sarka's movies on television as a child? Shy and I might have watched some of them together. I have a vague conviction that I enjoyed his film work, but have trouble remembering when and where I saw them. Did you see his movies on dates?"

He didn't know for sure whether he watched them with Shy? A likely story.

"Hell, yes," I answered. "I tracked down those Friday night revival houses, took dates to his films, and loved every one of them. Nothing like a horror movie with some good jump scares for teenage dating. They restore primitive gender roles. Women don't like horror films that scare their male dates. Men don't like horror films *unless* they scare their female dates."

"Right. And all this stuff about masturbation in our dreams tonight. . . . That smacks of teenage dating too, don't you think?"

Ah! So he was onto something after all. My rage began to subside.

"I hadn't noticed. But now that you mention it, I see what you mean."

"That could be the shared backstory of our dream suites. The only other explanation is that we have been the victims of a supernatural attack. Maybe the ghost of Faustian Benedek Sarka is preparing to offer us a deal."

We talked a bit more about that possibility. In the Black Ash Canyon case, I had found that having my mental privacy violated by a ghost was traumatically upsetting. After Herrera entered my mind, I felt violated, unclean, and weak. I saw now that some of my anger at Billy's dreams stemmed from my frightened refusal to entertain the possibility that tonight's dreams and sexual fantasies had not been entirely mine. A sickening thought. I began to feel slithery and unclean inside. But . . . they could be mine, made by trickster elves in the secret workshops of my unconscious. If they weren't, how had they managed to excite me so much?

I was blaming Steele for what I myself was doing: losing control of my sexuality. Billy wasn't crazed with desire. He was the partner I knew, the friend I trusted, the confidant I relied on.

Soon he padded off to bed.

I returned to the bedroom. Shy was awake. She wanted to know why I was having trouble sleeping. Before long she had coaxed from me a detailed account of my embarrassing dreams.

I talked and talked. She listened.

"Oh," she said when I had finished, "I think I can accommodate some of that. It fits with some of *my* sexual schemes."

I waited.

She laughed at me. "No need to frown, darling." I guess I must have been frowning, but at least I wasn't frothing with rage. Her sweet laughter delighted me, as did her next words. "I'm strictly a one-man woman. I'm not into threesomes or cuckoldry!"

To be honest, a few of my several hundred sexual ideas (not among the ones I had just talked out with her) had veered in those directions. But I was ecstatic that hers had not. "Thank God for that. So what *do* you want?"

"I love your cock, Mike. Surely you know that? I'd like to play with it."

"What? Like a toy?" I suddenly remembered,

after uttering these words, that when I was a little boy my mother and father had referred to my penis as my "toy-toy." The term might have derived from something my toddler self had said. Then again, it might have descended down through the family—perhaps from Grandpa Wilbur.

"Play with it like it was a toy, *my* toy. Make it do what I want, how I want, and when I want. Why don't you lie back and relax?"

An offer I couldn't refuse. I felt completely in love with her.

Afterward we tried to sleep. Shy dropped right off. I felt such an overflowing joy that I could not trade the moment for unconsciousness. I went back to the deck glowing with contentment.

I stared seaward. A fairy highway of shimmering moonlight ran toward the horizon. It would have been strenuous to travel it. I wasn't about to sacrifice my languor. So I let my imagination do the exploring, gathering impressions that began to dissolve the moment they were made.

Some while later I saw, or imagined I saw, a naked woman suspended above the swells just outside our cove. Slowly she sank down until the oily water closed over her head.

In my drowsy mind I heard one of the songs on Billy's homemade CD. It was the Robert Gordon and Link Wray version of that old rock 'n roll ghost story, *Endless Sleep*.

I looked at the sea and it seemed to say,
I took your baby from you away.
I heard a voice cryin' in the deep,
Come join me baby in my endless sleep.
Endless sleep.
Endless sleep.
Endless sleep.

I wasn't frightened. It could be worse, I remember thinking. Joining your baby in an endless sleep? That might mean a whole lot of dreams.

CHAPTER FOUR

Tuesday morning I awoke from another brazen dream. It seemed to begin with pressure on my prostate. I was bent over a table. A piece of wood sculpture rested on the far end. It depicted a horned figure with goat-like legs and a smiling but somehow wicked face. I thought of the god Pan. Someone behind me was slowly and methodically buggering my anal canal. I knew who the buggerer was. "Wait for it, wait for it," Billy Steele kept whispering. Solly Barlow knelt next to me, rubbing my neck and shoulders. "You're going to be fine, Mike," he intoned in a quiet voice. "You're on the right track. There's a gusher coming. Some of that white oil, some of that silver gold. That's what the doctor ordered." I could not see beneath the table, but I knew that my cock nestled in a mouth. It had to be Shy's mouth. I wanted it to be Shy's mouth.

What had gotten into me?

There wasn't much time to reflect on this shocking and abhorrent dream. Dreams in any case disperse instantly and angrily whenever we try to grasp them. The above account is a reconstruction I consider my best—on what grounds I have no idea.

As I sat on the edge of the bed, gathering myself,

Shy was putting on her finishing touches in the bathroom. She told me of the current mini-crisis. When Billy returned to his room after our tête-à-tête on the deck last night, Solly was gone. Billy figured he had slipped out for a walk. There was no trace of him this morning, however. Billy was over at the mansion, and we were supposed to meet him there.

The dream floated over my mind as I dressed and washed up. It was in line with yesterday's dreams, and familiar in that sense. Yet in another way the dream felt like an alien creation. Until one day ago, I didn't have dreams like this. Something really *had* gotten into me.

As we walked to the mansion, I consulted with my grandfather.

"Has some kind of ghost or spirit entered my mind?"

"No."

"I just can't believe these dreams come only from myself."

"They don't, but no entity has trespassed on your mental grounds. It's more like a Sending than a visit."

"A Sending? From a wizard?"

"The usual wizard's Sending would be an object or an animal meant to annoy or injure the recipient. What you have been getting in your sleep is more like a probe. It brings a clump of ideas and images. It then witnesses and makes some kind of record of how you make use of

those ideas and images. Some you run with. Some you
shun. Some you modify."

"*I get it. The probe reports back to the Sender. I'm*
being tested. Weighed and measured."

"*I think so."*

"*On another matter. When Dad was a boy, did you*
call his penis 'toy-toy'?"

"*Heavens, Mike. I would prefer not to talk about pe-*
nises."

"*Touchy! So you won't say?"*

"*I would prefer not to."*

I felt the immediate yawning absence that
marked the end of a Wilbur conversation.

Marta let us in with warm greetings and, to our
surprise, brief hugs. We followed the jolly housekeeper into her kitchen. Solly was in there, ruddy
and chipper, sipping coffee from a mug labeled
"Sarka Steel Board of Directors" as he held forth
on the main downgrades in contemporary America, its journalists in particular. "These TV pundits,
all they do is react to some asinine poll or specu-
late about a vague trend identified by some
pisspot prophet writing for a stuffy journal designed to be read on Sunday mornings by ever-
watchful Washington insiders. And the anchors!
So full of sanctimony about their precious service
to democracy. Hell, in Europe they call them
'newsreaders.' That's all the suckers really do, just

read us the frigging news. For that their commer-
cial-choked viewers owe them a tip of the cap? A
kneel down? A bow of the head?" Billy sat across
from him, nodding every now and then in a dis-
tracted way. That was all the fuel Solly needed to
keep the rant going. Marta asked our preferences
in eggs, then motioned for us to join our colleagues.

It was a fun breakfast. Solly lost the thread before long, and began exchanging lingering glances
with Marta. He was clearly cock of the walk this
morning. The rest of the Ghost Killers had no
doubts about where Solly had been late last night.
All of us, it seemed, were suddenly in thrall to
sexual urges.

"What's this Wagner Summers like?" Billy
wanted to know.

She shrugged. "He's a lawyer. Very particular."

"But aside from that."

"Mr. Sarka knew him for years. But they rarely
socialized. Summers is very active in local politics.
He serves on the boards of many institutions in
this area." Marta turned to Solly. "I have seen
him on those news shows you admire so much,
Solomon. He's a popular panelist."

"A born-to-inform type," Solly grumbled. "I already don't like him."

I asked Marta about the cave paintings in Folly's Cove. "Are they still visible?" she asked. Cheyenne and I nodded. "Allegra did them maybe six months before she drowned. I need hardly tell you that this family seems to be cursed in the fates of its women. Allegra Sarka immediately regretted the paintings and tried her best to wash them away, which proved to be a difficult chore. I have not seen them for years. I never go to the beach now. But I remember being impressed at their stubbornness. I clean things for a living, after all. Whatever the pictures meant to Allegra, she had made a landmark of it, and the landmark was not about to be washed away."

This new information changed the paintings for me. They were not, as I had first beheld them, an original vision. They were probably the result of a Sending very like the one that had detonated our dreams. Their existence marked a stage in Allegra's sexual decline, a prelude to her reckless affair with the passing yachtsman and ultimately her suicide. For me, they now represented a clear warning. Giving in to the lust probe, whatever its source, had indelible consequences.

I looked at Shy. I had poured my Sending-inspired thoughts into her open loving ears last night. Was she herself racked with filthy dreams later on? I bet she was. Something in her expression said she was. This case had taken a turn toward the dire.

Wagner Summers arrived. He was a thin, bespectacled man in a dapper tan suit, carrying a large brown leather briefcase. He greeted us with brusque efficiency. Wagner might have been a decent, well-meaning fellow. But our first impression was poisoned by the four people he had brought along with him.

"Let me introduce you to your fellow professionals," Summers began. "This is Roger Drivell and his select team of ghost hunters. Mr. Drivell has a great deal of experience with supernatural phenomena in Ventura and surrounding areas. Perhaps you know his books? They are considered standard works in the field. At Mr. Sarka's suggestion, I have hired them to work with you as needed in disarming the occult items in his estate. Better safe than sorry, right? Having two distinguished teams of supernatural investigators doubles our chances for a smooth transition."

Drivell looked like a composite of roles played in the 1940s by Turhan Bey—a phony swami, an occult scholar, the Amazing Mr. X. He had wavy gray hair, neatly combed, and a triangular goatee to obscure his weak chain. The hair frame set the stage for his bushy black eyebrows, which had been dyed jet black. His right hand sported a heavy black onyx ring. Solly, Cheyenne, and I got a quick once-over. He seemed to recognize Billy, though, and would glance at him when certain that Billy's attention was elsewhere.

"I feel ghost vibes," Roger Drivell announced to no one in particular as he rubbed his hands together, anticipating pleasure. "They start in the lower spine and move upward. It's my psychic self, you know. I'm very in tune with it. Gotta keep those lovin' good vibrations happening, as Brian Wilson says! This is going to be a most productive day."

Right off the bat I knew that Billy had been right about the guy. He spoke with the total self-approval of the very stupid.

His team consisted of two young men, Tag MacFarland and Chip Baggett, and a mature bottle-blonde. Tag and Chip wore black ball caps with the phrase "Drivell Ghost Hunts" in spikey green letters. They were weighed down with shoulder bags holding Electric Voice Phenomena recorders, camcorders equipped with night vision lenses, various Electro Magnetic Field meters, motion sensors, laser grids, and thermal cameras. Chip had one of those new computer watches from the successors to Steve Jobs, with Apps linking its tiny screen to his other electronic equipment. The busy little thing must have had some posture improvement program too, because every fifteen minutes a stirring phrase from the climax to the *1812 Overture* chimed out from a hidden mini-speaker in the watch, and a female voice said "Stop slouching. Stop slouching" in an oddly fetching tone. He fiddled with the smart watch's tiny buttons and miniature menus, but was unable to stop the posture improver from doing its thing.

Nothing was going to get past these guys. They immediately began placing their cameras, stationing their sensors, and taking readings with their numerous meters. I'll take this for their methods: they found the right place. The door to the turret rooms yielded readings that the boys considered remarkable. "Check this!" Tag exclaimed. "Look at those magnetic traces. Something came by here an hour ago." Chip pulled out a thermal device and held it against the door. "Cold in there too. Several degrees colder than on this side."

Bianca, the bottle-blonde, was the Drivell group's medium. She was a reasonably attractive woman, and I enjoyed a bantering conversation with her.

"I thought Dribble's wife Nellie served as his medium?"

"Semi-retired at this point. I'm afraid you're stuck with me."

"The only Bianca I know is in *Kiss Me, Kate!*"

"Very good! You know your stuff."

"And your last name, lest Papa spanka, Bianca?" I really had to watch myself more carefully. Stop slouching, Mike Buckman, stop slouching.

"Zitnik."

"Oh my. Really?"

"It has nothing to do with complexion. Mine is a good Czech name meaning 'one who bakes rye bread.'"

"There would be no good pastrami sandwiches without zitnik. Are you sensing any presences in this house?"

"Right now just yours."

Soon after that I broke it off with Bianca. Flirting, too, was a warning sign. Stop slouching.

Roger Drivell spoke to Billy about *Surveyor of Hell*. He liked the book, but found its passages about ghost theory to be over his head. Solly had been ejected from his perch in the kitchen, where Summers was having words with Marta about the dinner she had planned for this evening. The former cock of the walk looked on skeptically as Chip touted the virtues of his new computer watch. Time passed. Promptly at noon Robert Sarka arrived.

The heir apparent was a handsome devil, muscular and well-groomed. Dark hair, almond skin, and a classic aquiline nose testified to his Italian mother. He wore soft white slacks below a colorful orchid-print Hawaiian shirt. Casual in his attire, his brown eyes darted apprehensively about the corners of the house and he seemed to have trouble concentrating on the unfamiliar people who gathered around him to make his acquaintance and shake his hand. Marta greeted him with an enthusiastic embrace. Tears trickled down her cheeks. "To have you here again, after all these years! This is your home now, Robby. Your home!"

"I don't know about that," Sarka said, holding back. "But it is good to see you again, Marta, and looking so well."

Summers appeared, announcing that he and Robby had some business to discuss, and marched the new arrival into the office at the back of the house.

Marta had told us about Robby's career over breakfast. It began during college with an internet company selling stylish UV-protected clothing. From there he had branched out to a network of sites intended to attract serious collectors. These were niche-defined internet marketplaces, containing expert essays and historical materials, for collectors of American political buttons, British book bindings, ceramic cats, cigar paraphernalia, Bakelite jewelry, hood ornaments, antique yard fountains, and so on. These cyber marketplaces successfully wooed customers who had previously purchased their collection pieces on sites like EBay and ioffer. People liked their cozy specificity. They were designed for particular collectors, not for buyers in general.

Ten years ago Sarka launched his most ambitious enterprise, Fantasy Fantasy. Subscribers paid the website an annual fee entitling them to choose from a list of identities, such as American Spy, FBI Agent, Athletic Superstar (tennis, football, baseball, soccer, or golf) , Politician, Talk Show Host, News Analyst, Porn Star, Novelist, Professor (oceanography, history, ethnic studies, global warming science), CEO, Astronaut, and so on. For three months the subscriber lived inside a complex occupational game constructed by Robby's expert programmers. At the end of the game players received an elaborate assessment of their strengths and weaknesses in living out their particular fantasy. Several career counselors had recommended the game as a way for young people to straighten out their characteristic uncertainties. Bloggers had speculated about this latest form of cyber distraction. Politicians had talked about regulating certain problematic features of the Fantasy Fantasy games. Robby had struck it rich.

Wagner Summers called us to the conference

table in the back office. Robby sat to his right next to Marta. Summers had a pile of papers before him, and began to read Benedek Sarka's last will and testament.

Though written in customary legalese, the will seemed straightforward enough. The main beneficiary, as expected, was Robert Sarka. His father's bank accounts, investments, and other assets passed to him. He inherited a controlling block of shares in Sarka Steel International, together with several subsidiary companies. He inherited Folly's Cove, the main mansion and the guest quarters, and all of their contents. The theatrical company devoted to Christopher Marlowe's plays, Faustus Productions, its sets and costumes and all financial holdings, was divided equally among three veteran performers. Marta Barabas received 500K. Benedek hoped she would stay on, adequately compensated, to oversee the family mansion. There were lesser but generous bequests to the chief gardener and the head of the property's beach maintenance crew.

Certain of Benedek Sarka's possessions were deemed valuable enough to be expressly itemized in the will. Among these was a collection of films, most of them rare silents. My ears pricked up at the list of the three rarest of these prints. Marta cleaned things for a living. I was a trained film scholar, employed and tenured at the American Film Institute in Hollywood. There had always been rumors of fantastic cinematic treasures, such as the lost 8-hour version of *Greed* or Sternberg's missing masterpiece *The Case of Lena Smith*, now invisibly at rest in private collections. So I heard the brief list of the cream of Sarka's collection with considerable interest. Which movies had this decidedly peculiar man rescued from oblivion?

The first mentioned was a perfect copy of Tod Browning's *London by Night*. My jaw dropped. This horror film was one of the many great collaborations between Browning and the famous actor Lon Chaney. Officially no one living had ever seen the movie, but the makeup Chaney created for a leering vampire was now world famous through still photographs taken during the original production. This print was said to have been purchased from Browning's estate upon his death in 1962. This film alone, should its existence be made public, would be considered a momentous discovery, one of the most remarkable ever in the world of silent horror.

The second title was the *The Magician* from 1926. I knew the film well, and it had turned up in my recent researches into black magic. I knew why Sarka had coveted this title.

It was about a wicked magician trying to create

life. The dream of producing a homunculus by means of magical forces went back to the second part of Wolfgang Goethe's *Faustus*, the major retelling of the Faust legend during the Romantic period. Jack Parsons, the Satanist rocket scientist of the Ordo Templi Orientis, had been trying to create a magical child when he hired L. Ron Hubbard to be his scribal assistant.

The Magician was based on an early Somerset Maugham novel about a sorcerer named Oliver Haddo, whom the author based loosely on Aleister Crowley. In fact, Crowley himself had reviewed the Maugham novel under the name Oliver Haddo, and had accused the author of plagiarizing from Crowley's numerous published treatises on magic and the occult. Rex Ingram made the film in 1926, during the period when he was working out of a small studio in the south of France. The celebrated director Michael Powell, who as a young man had apprenticed himself to Ingram, was a member of the crew.

A young female virgin is captivated and corrupted by Oliver Haddo. In the end he takes her to his castle, where he plans to murder her for her heart's blood, which a magician must have in order to create new life. Her former lover intervenes. Haddo's magical laboratory burns. For a brief spell the film is tinted red. This is one of several moments where the magic of cinematography serves the Gothic atmosphere of *The Magician*. In a dream sequence, Haddo is transformed into a most disturbing image of the god Pan (a favorite of Crowley, whose most famous piece of writing is the poem "Hymn to Pan").

Apparently there had been plans for more color experiments. Sarka's print of *The Magician* had been owned by the admired cinematographer John Seitz, who for personal reasons left Ingram's French operation and returned to Hollywood after completing *The Magician*. As a memorial to their collaborations, Ingram and Seitz had designed a highly tinted and toned version of their movie and had two copies made to their detailed specifications by the highly respected technicians at Handshiegl (a company soon to be absorbed by Technicolor). Again, this was an astounding find. Legions of horror fans had always championed this movie. If they heard about this new print, there would be excitement yet again.

The third film was another lost movie, earlier than the other two. It was Universal's legendary *Three Queens*, released in 1918 to capitalize on publicity concerning the murder of its writer-director, Pierre Trevain, whose body was found on the Universal City lot with a smashed skull in 1917, just before completion of his first and only

88

movie. The film starred J. Warren Kerrigan. An actress named Pearl Seagrove played a small but important role in the second section of the movie, shot in the charming village of Rio Vista on the Sacramento River. This was her final movie. After completing it she opened a chain of jewelry stores called The Pearly Gates and crafted pieces in her characteristic style, beautiful and witty, now avidly sought by collectors. One of Robby Sarka's collector sites was devoted to her work. Barbara DeLure played the starring role of a mysterious and fatal vampire who enters the hero's life in different guises at three different time periods. Art was imitating life. DeLure was later identified as Trevain's murderer; their linked biographies, which obsessed the Hollywood press corps for several months, bore clear resemblances to the plot of Trevain's movie.

Because of the writer-director's untimely death, the film had to be finished by Warren Kerrigan's twin brother, the production manager Wallace Kerrigan. In shooting and editing the final scenes of *Three Queens*, he displayed an unexpected Gothic flair that several early critics considered a benchmark in fantastic cinema. Kerrigan had previously shaped early documentaries for the American Film Manufacturing Company in Santa Barbara, but sadly, after the concluding third of

Three Queens, he never directed again. Sarka's copy of the movie could be traced back to the private holdings of the Universal executive Izzy Bernstein.

At this point the lawyer called for a break. Summers fingered a small cigar as he headed for the terrace.

Billy asked me about the estate's film collection. "Why do you suppose Benedek went for silent films? I expected that there would be items from his own career."

"He was an actor, of course. Prints show up in the estates of directors, producers, and cinematographers, but not usually in the collections of stars. They have other keepsakes and mementoes— costumes, props, annotated scripts. But they don't as a rule handle or work with film itself. They aren't usually involved in final cuts and things of that ilk."

"OK. So his memorabilia would probably not include actual films. He bought these items as a collector rather than acquiring them in natural circumstances. How do you explain the preference for silents?"

"Maybe it had to do with those early films he made. I'm guessing that they were elaborate home movies, and did not have had sound tracks. There are special complexities in editing a film with a recorded soundtrack. It could also be that he just preferred eerie silent films to eerie sound films. Kenneth Anger, a Crowleyan filmmaker, said that the silent period had a kind of 'extra magic.' A silent image, he went on to say, is more like a ghost or a dream."

"Interesting."

"We'll have to cut this short, Billy. I need to make a call. I'll be somewhere in the front yard. See you soon."

I went out and punched in the number of William Kerrigan in Santa Maria, CA. He was the author of the *Video Watchdog* essay on Benedek Sarka. I had done a little research on him. Kerrigan was a former academic who earned considerable respect as an interpreter of the works of John Milton and William Shakespeare. He was also the grandson of Wallace Kerrigan, the man who had filmed the final scenes of *Three Queens*, and the grand-nephew of J. Warren Kerrigan. I was banking on him knowing a few things that could help us with the Sarka case.

The phone rang. I sat down on a wooden bench in the shade beneath a group of sheltering palms.

"Hello," said a deep male voice.

"Hello. I'm Mike Buckman of the Ghost Killers, and I'm doing a job for—"

"Thanks, but I'm not—"

"Wait! Slow down. I'm not marketing any- thing. I'm doing a job for the estate of Benedek Sarka." I tried, under pressure from the man's roiling impatience, to provide him with some context.

"Listen, Mike. We're all cogs in a vast machine. We're not altogether sure what the machine is trying to accomplish. We do our little jobs, and we know no higher wisdom. Right now one of my jobs is writing fiction. I'm on the fourth chapter of a new mystery. A toe of mine gives me trouble and today is hurting quite smartly, but the writing was going better than could be expected until you interrupted me. Exactly what do you want?"

"I want to ask you about your grandfather Wal- lace and Benedek Sarka."

"As you obviously know already, I've written on Sarka. I'm not aware of any connection be- tween him and Grampa Wally."

A commotion of some kind had broken out in the mansion. I heard raised voices. Focusing on my call, I told Kerrigan about the print of *Three Queens* in the Sarka estate.

"Man! Grampa Wally was particularly fond of Izzy Bernstein. When he left, the studio lost its appeal so far as Wally was concerned. Universal, of course, is notorious for their half-hearted efforts in the area of film preservation. I never saw a ray of hope for *Three Queens*. Man, I would *love* to see that movie."

I promised him that I would try my best to arrange a showing for him. But right now, what I needed above all was to pick his brain on the subject of Benedek Sarka.

"You have my attention. What do you want to know?"

"Did Sarka have anything to do with the Pasadena OTO?"

"I found an obscure OTO journal called *Oriflamme* where Grady McMurtry, who took over the organization in the 1970s, wrote that he considered Sarka a 'fellow traveller.' The phrase implies, I think, that Sarka was an occultist but not a member of the OTO. I don't think he was a member of any magical lodge."

McMurtry had appeared in my own researches. He had joined the Pasadena OTO after meeting Jack Parsons in 1941, and soon graduated from his ROTC unit to become a Second Lieutenant in the United States Army. "But McMurtry did *know* him?"

"Possibly. Sarka was of course a celebrity. McMurtry might have been referring to Sarka's work as a film actor."

"Why do you think Sarka was so drawn to Marlowe?"

"First of all, because of his obvious interest in the Faust legend. Marlowe's work is a short parade of horror. It has, besides Mephistophilis carrying out Faust's damnation, Islamic conquerors, a Machiavellian mass murderer, Catholics slaughtering Huguenots, and Edward II's oddly passive death at the hands of a killer named Lucifer. Marlowe was an old love. Benedek had seen that famous production at the Torch Theatre near Hyde Park Corner directed by a teenage Peter Brook. Probably he had never felt so cutting edge, so close to the heart of things. Did you know that Brook had engaged Aleister Crowley himself as the production's 'Occult Advisor'?"

I actually gulped. "No, I didn't know that."

"Crowley was a man of some substance, you know. He loved Milton. I've tried to imagine how *Paradise Lost* appeared to Crowley's eyes. He must have found deep enchantment in the poem's cosmic stage, interstellar flights, detailed angelology and demonology, account of creation, and so forth. Above all, I think Crowley must have thrilled to the sense throughout Milton's poem of penetrating beyond mortal limits to behold divine beings and founding events. On one of his attempts to climb K2 in Pakistan, Crowley was told that he would have to shed his packet of poetry books for the last leg of the ascent. He refused, saying 'I cannot abandon Milton.'

"But in 1942 he was seriously in decline—broke, almost friendless, hopelessly addicted to heroin. You've probably seen the pictures. Bald, thickened, jowly, big caverns under his eyes. The eyes still look pretty powerful. He was famous from youth for his boring stare. That was about all he had going for him toward the end. What it actually meant for Brook to appoint him Occult Advisor on his *Doctor Faustus* was smuggling the old magus into Oxford, where Crowley instructed the amateur cast on how to behave during the conjuring scenes. There weren't many reviews. But we know the actors were casually and shockingly blasphemous. Mephistophilis played all the Seven Deadly Sins, and I imagine he evoked Christ-like postures to illustrate them, a Crucifixion look with the head bowed to illustrate Vanity—that sort of thing. Brook came from a scientific family. But he respected magic. He made a famous remark about the need to create magic from the resources of a theatre. I think he wanted the occult side of the play to be as powerfully realistic as he could make it. Enter Crowley."

The dust-up in the house had reached a conclusion of sorts. The front door opened, and the Drivell Ghost Hunters, acting angry and misused, walked toward a black Lincoln Voyager in the paved parking area.

"Crowley keeps coming up," I told Kerrigan.

"He does in anything occult. There haven't been many new discoveries in magic, you know. Crowley wrote about almost everything in the field, Tarot cards, Eastern sex practices, all the traditions of conjuring, drugs, the works. Timothy Leary said he modeled his repellent mantra "Turn on. Tune in. Drop out." on the sayings of Crowley. Reading a Crowley biography is among other things a good test of the strength of your stomach. He devised a communion wafer for his Gnostic Mass that was laced with sperm and menstrual blood. He did many stomach-wrenching things. He was also interested in fecal matter, about which I will only say a little more.

"Crowley once remarked that all worlds are excremental. I thought a lot about that one. It goes back to Christian theology. God is everything, therefore something must be taken out of God, made separate from him, in order for our world to be created. The world is in a sense God's sperm, God's excrement. Milton has a lovely passage where the Holy Spirit 'dove-like sat'st brooding on the vast abyss and mad'st it pregnant.' I think Crowley had that in mind.

"I suppose young Benedek Sarka met the old bastard when attending *Doctor Faustus* at the Torch

Theatre in London. I'm saying that Marlowe, for Sarka, was through and through contaminated with Crowley. A devotion to one was a devotion to the other."

Kerrigan paused. "Is that about it?" he asked rhetorically.

"I guess so. This has been tremendously useful."

"I'm happy to hear that, Mike. My parents called me Mike. At home I was always Mike or Michael Kerrigan. Good luck to your team. Sounds like you're going to need it."

"Good luck with the book."

I hit the off button.

When I got back to the house, Solly, Billy, Wagner Summers, and Robby Sarka were jawing in the back office. Shy came into the living room and filled me in. Tag and Chip had raised a ruckus, claiming to have seen a shadowy form walk through the turret door. The dials on their meters and sensors were hopping. Roger Drivell, declaring that his team had just made a major discovery, demanded that the door be unlocked. His main concern was to capture the spirit on a digital camcorder.

In the meantime, Summers returned to the office and discovered that one of his papers was missing.

Before Robby received the occult pieces of his inheritance, Benedek Sarka had instructed the lawyer to give his son a letter. It had to be read before the unlocking of the turret. The envelope containing this letter, headed "Last Advice for My Son," had disappeared.

This was the first the Ghost Killers had heard of such a letter. Billy questioned Summers on whether he had told the Drivell team of its existence. The lawyer tried being non-committal, expressing outrage at being questioned in this manner, but Steele kept grilling him. Summers finally admitted that Drivell himself, and only Drivell, had been told. Billy shifted from Summers to Drivell. Had he spoken to his team about the letter? Drivell insisted vehemently that he had not.

Billy went back to interrogating Summers. The lawyer had said that his hiring of the Drivell Ghost Hunters was approved by Benedek Sarka. Was that true? Had not Summers hired Drivell all by himself, thinking that the Drivell people, being natives of Ventura and having done many favors for local residents and businesses seeking an economic return on their supposed ghosts, would be more likely than the Ghost Killers to take direction from Counselor Summers? The lawyer never really confessed to these charges. He fell into silence, though, and the silence was eloquent.

Billy suggested that the Drivell Ghost Hunters be searched. At this point Drivell gathered his forces and huffed off.

When Shy and I entered the office, Summers was shaking his head. "I'm not sure what to do. The will is clear that Robert must read that letter before being given the keys to the turret rooms. But the letter is gone. Eventually, of course, if it remains lost, I will hand over the keys to you, Robert. But I'm reluctant to do that right now."

"You can stop worrying, Mr. Summers," I told him. "I think I know where the letter is. I'll take some time this afternoon to gather my thoughts and look into a few things. I suggest that we enjoy Marta's delicious dinner this evening. After that, I'll go out by myself for a while, and bring the letter back with me. Tomorrow morning we can explore the turret room. Good enough?"

The lawyer smiled. "Good enough!" Established protocol was back in place.

It was dark by the time I found the address on Oak Ridge Drive and parked the Creep Jeep at the curb in front. The house was small. There wasn't much in the way of landscaping.

The door opened soon after my knock. Bianca Zitnik stood before me in cut-off jeans and a halter top, an ironic smile on her face. "I figured it would be you. Come on in."

I knew it was her by a simple process of elimination.

Who stole the letter? The Ghost Killers? No possible motive. Robby Sarka? Ridiculous. He was, after all, about to receive the letter from his father's lawyer. Wagner Summers? No likely motive. Marta Barabas? She had just inherited a half a million bucks. No apparent motive. That left the Drivell group. The only one with half a brain was Bianca Zitnik. She had a possible motive, and I thought I knew what it was. Eliminate the seriously unlikely, and the most plausible explanation left, no matter how implausible, is probably the one.

She offered me a drink. I asked for a scotch and soda, and she returned with one for each of us. I sat in a rattan armchair. She was next to me on the end of a sofa.

"I settled on you as my likely tracker," she began, "by a process of elimination. You seemed to be the smartest guy in the house."

"I don't know if that's true, but thanks for the compliment."

She picked up an envelope from the coffee table in front of her, and handed it to me. "I was going to return this letter tomorrow morning after looking it over. Eric and Tag enjoyed their maiden effort at playacting. They get bored to death horsing around with those phony baloney gadgets that Drivell buys for them. The kids agreed to help me out. Drivell didn't know a thing, which is his usual state."

"I take it you had a relationship with Benedek Sarka."

"Oh yes. For five years we had a long and winding affair. At one point toward the end he was writing that letter to his son Robert, and kept joking about all the lascivious secrets he was revealing. He laughed at how outraged his tight-assed son would be to learn of our escapades. When Benny died, I really began to worry about it. I wanted to know if there were embarrassing passages in that letter, and if so, how embarrassing. Then I learned that Roger had gotten this lucrative gig at the Sarka Mansion. We've known each other for years, and worked together on various supernatural matters. It was no problem persuading him to hire me as the team medium. An oracular comment or two, some observations about the energy in the room. That's enough for Roger. He doesn't really *want* any more than that."

"I assume you've looked through the letter."

"I skimmed it. Nothing about me. The whole thing was much ado about nothing."

We beat around the bush for a while, but soon she started telling me what I wanted to know. There wasn't any point in further concealment. She knew her little transgression would not be prosecuted. Bianca's plan had succeeded perfectly. She wanted knowledge, wanted to be prepared for the worst. She had that knowledge, and her mind was at peace.

"Tell me about Sarka. I take it he had some unusual interests."

Benedek Sarka and Bianca Zitnik had indeed, on their long and winding road, visited some strange places. But the most unusual thing about Sarka as a bedroom partner was the sheer intensity of his lust. For Benny it was sex, sex, sex, sex all the way through. If there was anything outside of sex, it was power power power, power all the way through. Sex and power were two sides of the same thing. Sarka was a sex and power maniac.

"Do you mind telling me some of things you did?"

"He liked to read pornography to me, particularly stuff by the sorcerer Aleister Crowley. A book called *White Stains*. A poem about a woman named Binetti, I think. Some of this was fun, but some of it was just disgusting. I remember a super raunchy bit of doggerel called 'Leah Sublime,' which Benny called the dirtiest poem ever written.

And hey, cowboy, I haven't read all the poems ever written, not by a long shot, but I'm sure he was right.

"Sex itself was like performing a rite. He liked language from Revelations in the Bible, and when we were going at it would start calling me his Scarlet Woman or his Whore of Babylon. When he was in an affectionate mood, he would call me Alostrael. He said that meant the grail or womb of God. We took drugs. His favorites were peyote, cocaine, heroin. But he kept the dosages at a moderate level, as if he were pacing himself over the long haul. Benny was seventy-five years old at the end of our affair, and remarkably vigorous. He liked to do things that took hours, sometimes all day, to finish. One time he had me bring him to the edge of orgasm over and over and over. I was supposed to do and say anything and everything I could think of to arouse him, but never let him cum. After hours of this he became semi-incoherent. After more hours of this he started falling asleep. It was then my job to awaken him, or *almost* awaken him. Finally, in a comatose trance, he ejaculated in one long steady stream. Damnedest thing I've ever seen. Benny said later that he saw incredible visions, merged with the universe. He loved that kind of mumbo-jumbo. On these special day-long cums of his, he would

always eat his sperm and brag about how powerful it made him.

"Poor Benny. He was after a satisfaction that
cannot be found on this earth."

"Could you elaborate on that?"

She shrugged. "Flesh is flesh. The body can only do so much. Delay it, complicate it, enhance it
with drugs, but the end-pleasure comes, and that's
it. That wasn't enough for Benny."

"You seem to have enjoyed him."

"Yeah, I did, I admit it. You never knew what
was coming next. Sometimes we could only use
our mouths to excite each other. Sometimes it was
all back door stuff. Sometimes it was the good old
straight missionary business. All sorts of combina-
tions. He never ran out of ideas. Like I said, for
this man it was sex sex sex and power power
power, all the way from his top to his core. He
was shameless. He made it a life's work to be
shameless."

There were more details to come, but Bianca had
pretty much said her piece.

When I got back to the guest cottage at Folly's
Cove, Shy was lying in bed reading a book. I put
the envelope on the night stand.

"You really did bring it back. I'm impressed,"
Shy said, putting her book aside. "Did you get

Bianca's story?"

I told her the gist of it, leaving out most of the sexual detail.

"Boy, talk about a demon lover! Bianca had her hands full. Benny wasn't about to give up coffee for Sanka."

"Good one. I tried a Cole Porter joke on her this afternoon. I think it impressed her."

"Was she interested in you?"

"A little, maybe. She certainly enjoys talking about sex. Sarka seems to have talked about little else." Then finally I was able to pose the question I had been meaning to ask her all day long. "I'm curious, Shy. Did you have sexual dreams last night?"

She made a face. I call it her smiling frown.

"I did. In the beginning I was staring at the cave paintings, especially the sexual one. The way my dreams go, whenever I see a group of people I just plunge right into whatever they're doing. That's what happened in my dream last night. But there was only one female in that painting. I guess my mind didn't find that role, as painted, very appealing, because when I plunged in, the two men were pleasuring me."

"Who were the two men?"

Her eyebrows folded down, making a scowl of disapproval. "Must you?"

"'Fraid so. I think something is screwing with our dreams and sexual thoughts."

She stared at me, then blurted it out. "You and Billy."

I didn't ask her who was doing what. Who cared? Those details didn't matter. I wondered for a moment if there were two separate Sendings, one for each gender. The cave paintings were more prominent in her dreams than in mine or Billy's. Moreover, those paintings were the creations of a woman—a woman visited by a Folly's Cove Sending. These thoughts also seemed pointless. The main absolute in my world was Cheyenne Griswold Buckman. She had been touched by a spell. That was the main thing. A ball of scumbag thoughts and images had bonded with her precious mind and was now unfolding there. The quicker I got to the bottom of this business the better it would be for my wife and me, for the Ghost Killers. All of us were infected. A section of our minds had been lost to erotic frenzy.

"I'm going to work for a bit, darling. I'll come to bed soon."

On my way out I picked up the envelope. Earlier I had decided not to read it. But now my mind had changed.

CHAPTER FIVE

I read the Sarka letter, and put in another hour of internet research before going to bed. There was of course a new round of distressing dreams. They had some heterosexual elements, but their hot core was increasingly homosexual. I thought I knew why.

Locating an electric waffle iron in one of the kitchen cabinets, Billy made breakfast. I let my mind wander after a sip of coffee, and it began to ring changes on last night's sexual imagery. The alien dream thoughts were increasingly at home, like wild animals becoming house-broken. Now the big cats purred at the breakfast table.

Last night I had scanned the letter into my computer. I passed the machine around to my colleagues. When everyone finished it, I called Robby Sarka at the main house to invite him over. Giving in to Marta's pleas, he had bedded down in the mansion last night.

He didn't keep us waiting. I seated him in the living room, and handed him the actual physical letter Bianca had returned to me, penned in Benedek's flowing hand. "This is of course addressed to you. I took the liberty of reading it, then showed it to the whole team. I suggest you read it now.

We'll be out on the deck, and will join you in a quarter hour or so."

Last Advice for My Son

We have not been "dear" to each other for many years, so I won't irritate you by beginning this last letter with conventional salutations.

You chose a business career over the artistic pathways explored by your mother and myself. Given that predilection, I wish you had devoted your talents and energies to Sarka Steel or its subsidiary companies. But you have always been insistent on your precious independence. With my death, of course, the controlling shares in Sarka Steel will pass to you. Will you sell them and use the money to grow your empire of internet diversions? Poor confused Robby, so certain that originality is his hope and not his curse. But alas, I have no other heir.

As you have every reason to expect, something else passes on as well. Blessing? Curse? He has been both of those to me. Like you, Baphomet is a businessman. He will want a deal. Running away, saying "no" to a deal, will not be allowed. Let me give you some advice. Baphomet and I have entered into many mutual pacts over the years. I have not always realized the full consequences of my obligations. But I tell you with perfect confidence that he has been completely fair and honest about what I was to give and get.

You have always blamed me for your mother's death. Baphomet at the time was still learning how to transfer his sexual will to a living consciousness in a way that the two could mate with each other. He wanted a willing submission, a conquest without overthrow. But he was having trouble sending these thoughts to a specific destination. Your mother began receiving transmissions intended for me. Even I found his communications at that time too powerful. They did not produce the ideal balance. I loved your mother deeply. She was a great treasure in all ways. But the Baphomet sexgrams were a disaster for her. Her death changed me forever. I turned all my rage against Baphomet. In the end I was able to bind him to devote every power at his command to the chore of self-control. He's improved somewhat. I also made it a precondition of our cooperation that he never place thoughts in *your* mind. That is the plain truth, son. The freedom you have consistently used to heap scorn on me was in truth my gift. I paid for it.

Don't ask Baphomet for the moon. You must consider his resources. He is not like Old Nick in the folktales or Mephistophilis in Marlowe's great tragic drama. He cannot give you great wealth. But then, you have that already, don't you? He cannot give you Helen of Troy, Ann Boleyn, Josephine, Vera Nabokov, the real-life models for *The Witches of Eastwick*, Doris Day, that Lewinski woman, or anyone else your wayward heart might consider doing a deal for. But he can bestow on you a powerful sexual charisma. The men and women best suited to your erotic tastes will be attracted to you. In exchange he will ask little—*very* little in my estimation. Just a certain sexual atmosphere (I suppose one could call it a "ritual" or a "procedure"), and a set of goals amounting to nothing more than the full exploration of your desires. Do what thou wilt, as Rabelais said. He said it too. Unlike Rabelais, he really meant it.

You will learn to appreciate that trait of his. Baphomet *means it*.

He can also give you his knowledge. I have made pacts concerning both of his main goods—sexual fulfillment and knowledge. You should give careful thought as to how you arrange these two ventures. I find that sexual exertion becomes, in old age, something of a chore. Oh, it is nice to know that I still have allures and charms, that I still am virile. But I confess that pools of disgust sometimes seep out from the bottom soil of my mind. Perhaps you might persuade him to feast on your sexual labors until you reach, say, sixty, and thereafter to compensate you in occult knowledge? The association between Baphomet and our family could be long-standing, and we Sarka males should be creative rather than hidebound in devising the contracts securing our cooperation.

I imagine that somewhere in that closed mind of yours you must be wondering what this "Baphomet," if there were a Baphomet, could do to you? Could he give you cancer? I honestly don't know. I have never made him angry enough to try. I have chosen cooperation. It might be a very bad idea to find out what he could do to you. For the controls he is under are not those of an ordinary being. Much the best course, my son, is to make a deal.

I met him in London in 1942. My father, with an eye on my future role in Sarka Steel International, had arranged for me to accompany him on a business trip to negotiate a munitions contract with the British government. Perhaps I had a touch of your rebelliousness in my soul. I found the arms negotiations impressive but tedious. I was just fourteen, after all. London only came alive for me when outside a pub I met two Oxford undergraduates welling with enthusiasm over the early successes of one of their schoolmates, Peter Brook. He was about to film a movie. The very next night his own production of *Doctor Faustus*, acted by Oxford undergraduates, would open at the Torch Theatre near Hyde Park Corner. Today so much has been written about this *Faustus* that it has acquired a grandeur in the historical imagination which it never attained in actuality. Tickets were sold door to door. The production played for three nights only, and was scarcely noticed in the press. Its most detailed notice appeared in the film journal *Sight and Sound*.

But it meant everything to me. My companions, who managed to smuggle me into the pub and order me a few rounds, gave me a ticket. On opening night, as the audience milled about the lobby before the curtain rose, I met Baphomet, whom Brook had appointed his production's "occult adviser." He was an old man, near the end of his earthly existence, but robust. He took a liking to me. I heard enchanting tales of his travels, his discoveries, his mountaineering, his hilarious and often prickly encounters with the rich and famous. We sat next to each other during the performance. He filled my ear with whispered comments about brilliant and bungled moments. Afterwards, in the locked bedroom of one of Brook's investors, he gently and considerately initiated me into the VII° magic he had devised for the Ordo Templi Orientis. Giving out mystical names was one of Baphomet's specialties. It was not mere designation, but rather a form of divining. He called me Sanctissimus Carnem or "Sacred Flesh." When I told him of my interest in improving the design of the motion picture camera, he fixed me with his eagle-like stare. "Will that remain your interest? I think not." How true was that thought! I had on that very night found a new set of fascinations.

Five years later I was contacted by an Air Force Lieutenant named Grady McMurtry. He offered me an extraordinary job. Many others had been considered for this task, but Grady assured me that my qualifications were unparalleled. I later learned that one of my rivals for this commission was a young Los Angeles filmmaker with a magical bent who called himself Kenneth Anger. Both of us could operate a motion picture camera. Both of us could process and edit film, make prints, and so on. Both of us admired Baphomet. But Anger had not been initiated into high esoterica by the master himself. Moreover, the World War was winding down. One prerequisite for this incredible job was an ability to gain entry to Great Britain in all conceivable circumstances. Anger, a nobody, could not claim such privilege. I, however, because of the importance of Sarka Steel to the Allied war effort, would always be admitted to England. I now feel that Anger being an openly practicing homosexual also spoke against his candidacy. Baphomet preferred my less finished, more malleable sexuality.

I accepted the job. The old seer was right. I would not long be famous for my technological prowess. I had in a way been hired for that, but my skills were metamorphosing. I invented a camera with a special wheel of lenses. I waited, on call.

In late November of 1947 the call came. I flew to London, where I hired a car to drive me to Netherworld, once a middle-class Victorian country residence, then a sprawling, ivy-covered boarding house in Hastings on the South Coast. A sign in the dining room read "Guests are requested not to tease the ghosts." For Baphomet, who was living there, I bore a package of delicacies from his many friends in California. (I did not tell him that they had referred to him, to my face, as "Old Crow.") I filmed for several days.

While at Netherworld, to my lifelong amusement, I learned of another of the rivals over whom I had triumphed. One of Baphomet's many trainees, a woman named Jean Schneider, worked in Hollywood as the housekeeper to *wunderkind* director Orson Welles. Initial signs were favorable. Jean wrote of her master's taste for magic. Baphomet himself dreamed of Welles serving him, and sent the young lion a play of his called *Mortadello* in the hope that Welles would film it after finishing his current project, a movie about some rich newspaperman. Welles, luckily for my sake, had loathed the drama. Soon thereafter, the spinning ball of Baphomet's will landed in my slot. Sixty-eight years later, I still find merriment in the idea that my film career began when I replaced the director of *Citizen Kane*.

You will find my movie, and Baphomet, in the third floor of my turret. Read this over again in a calmer frame of mind, my son. You will need to be calm.

Forgive my name-dropping. "Baphomet" is a name he took for himself while exploring the sexual magick now codified in the VII°, VIII°, IX°, X°, and XI° degrees of esoteric knowledge in the Ordo Templi Orientis system. He robed himself in many names. Ipsissimus. Perdurabo. To Mega Therion. The Beast 666. At various times in his life he passed as Count Vladimir Svareff, Prince Chioa Khan, Sir Alaster de Kerval, Dionysius Carr, Knaw Li Ya, Mahatma Guru Sri Parmahansa Shivaji, Rev. C. Verey, Count MacGregor, Leo Vincey. He was born Edward Alexander Crowley. He named himself Aleister.

Grady McMurtry commissioned the film with Crowley's full participation. Back in America I made the first print from the original negative. I watched it. I met the Crowley *spiritus*. As I have already discussed, he wanted my sexual energies in exchange for various favors. I was impressed at his powers. He is quite adept at demonstration, as you will soon realize.

I kept that first print for myself, and mailed McMurtry the next three, fully expecting that the Baphomet ghost would from the grave establish the same control over the Pasadena Agape Lodge he once enjoyed in life. But no. Mine was to prove a private revelation.

McMurtry thought my film satisfactory. The prints were clean and sharp. I expect they are still shown to advanced initiates in the OTO cult. But they had no magical properties. The

Crowley ghost is attached to only the first print made from the first pristine negative of the film I shot of his death. As a result of that, McMurtry regarded the filming as a failed experiment. He knew that Baphomet had wanted to come back, and in his haunting to achieve great eminence in the world.

That is indeed his goal. But Crowley no longer operates within the confines of the OTO. He now works through me, and soon through you.

I have loved you, son, but not in the modern way. Today we are to adore our offspring for their uniqueness, their unpredictable differences from their parents. How frivolous and defeatist is this modern unconditional love! I love you for your ability to forge a continuity, continue my wisdom, and replace me in the world. I love you because you can be more of me.

I look to the future. It's yours, and I love you for it. You must see why and how you matter to Crowley. Our destiny is to supply him with libidinal energy, which he sublimates to his higher magical tasks. We are the actual sensations of his lust—his power source. Baphomet will be forever. When he achieves his ultimate goals, our family's contribution will be honored and held sacred throughout the world. His eminence will be ours. Rejoice, my sweet Sanctissimus Carnem.

Yours sincerely,
Benedek Sarka

When we returned, Robby was sitting with his face cradled in his hands. His abominable letter, back in its envelope, sat on the coffee table before him. I couldn't read his expression, which to my eye shifted back and forth from dread to astonishment, then from astonishment back to dread, back and forth from the one to the other like the duck-rabbit in Wittgenstein's *Philosophical Investigations*.

We all took seats, and I addressed the room.

"Finally Robert knows what he has inherited. Finally we know what we have been hired to do. The ghost in the case is none other Aleister Crowley. Sarka was bound to this spirit. He defends his actions, and recommends that Robert continue to serve the Crowley ghost." I fixed my gaze on Robert. "I assume the Ghost Killers are still being asked to neutralize or destroy Aleister Crowley in his current form?"

"When Summers contacted you," Robby said, "I didn't know exactly what my father would pass on to me. I knew it involved a supernatural power. I knew the power was evil. On the day before she drowned Allegra told me that father had an 'evil partner,' as she put it, who was 'not of this world.' She believed that my father had allowed this evil partner to violate her in some way, push her into evil acts, torment her with unmanageable temptations. She had tried appealing to him. When mother made these charges directly to his face, so she told me, my father insisted that the promptings she so much resented were not personal. He was confident that her discomforts would be temporary. It was simply a matter of his partner learning to control his powers. She knew at that moment my father was either a liar or hopelessly deceived.

"Her story made my six-year-old heart yearn to save her! I begged her to leave him and take me with her. It was my duty. I didn't have an evil partner. I would be her good man. I wanted to save her so much that I began crying. As I imagined our future, sobbing because I wanted so much to shield her from father's corruption, she shook her head so violently that my tears dried out. I understood the strength of her bond with him. It stood before me like a mountain. She couldn't leave him. I mustn't ask that of her. She hadn't the power to do that.

"But *I* had to leave him, she commanded, at my earliest opportunity. Something might happen to her. One never knew the future. Whatever it held,

I was never again to trust my father's sincerity. He might offer me his love or his understanding or his help. But his highest obligation would always be to the evil partner. She was right. I've never doubted that. The letter proves she was right."

For Robby Sarka, the main burden of his father's last advice was vindication. His mother had been correct to warn him. He had been correct to heed her warning. Vindication was a nice thing for this troubled man to have, but it wasn't going to help us with the matter at hand. I had to refocus Robby on the problems facing us right now. "The Crowley ghost is still summoning those 'unmanageable temptations' your mother loathed. I assume that suicide was her only way of escaping them. Since we arrived here two days ago, unusual sexual ideas have been bubbling through our dreams and fantasies. I hope this isn't too personal, but didn't you have an erotic dream last night?"

The question embarrassed him. His head bent down. If he had been naked, he would have been staring at his penis. "So *that* was the evil partner. They were dreams about . . . varieties of masturbation."

"Look at me, Robby." I saw a child in his blushing, frightened face. He had been a tough child, though, and there was resolve in his face along with the shame. "Your father wrote that he had managed to protect you from the ghost's interference. That restraint became part of their binding agreement. With his death, however, the old arrangement no longer holds. All of us Ghost Killers began having those dreams on the night before you arrived. Now they have come to you, and are worming their way through your mind. I can assure you, on the basis of what has happened to us, that they will become stronger if you stay on this estate. They may get stronger in any case. In us, the sexual ideas in our dreams have begun to settle into our waking realities.

"So I have to ask you again. Just what do you want us to do? I don't know if we are strong enough to defeat this ghost. But we can't do anything without getting closer to it. We'll have to beard Crowley in his lair—get into the turret rooms, climb to the top, watch this obscene movie of his death and see what happens, just as your father recommends. Then we can assess his powers and weaknesses and proceed from there. You'll have to accompany us, I'm afraid. Crowley will expect that. You compliance is what he wants. I don't want to encounter an enraged Crowley who feels he has no chance of getting that.

"Two things, then, for you to consider, Robby. Are you strong enough to actually contact this evil partner your mother told you to flee? That appears to have been the key conversation in your entire life. Will you keep running away? Or do you want us to try to kill this ghost? If you do, our compensation will have to be renegotiated. The ghost in your turret in no run-of-the-mill spook. He was the most infamous and accomplished black magician of the modern era."

Robby nodded. "I understand about the payments. Look, I've just inherited something akin to the vaults of Uncle Scrooge. How much do you want?"

I looked around at the Ghost Killers. Billy shrugged. I thought it over. We were a confident bunch, but there was no soft-pedaling the danger of this undertaking. We were already paying a large psychological toll. What was it worth to have your fantasy life changed, quite possibly changed forever? We could argue over this for days. I had better be decisive. I remembered Sigmund Freud saying that a worthy psychoanalyst should never feel guilty about being well compensated.

"We'll want a million dollars each. That seems to me a reasonable sum for the risks we'll be taking. Should we succeed, there may in the future be charities and causes that we consider worthy of financial support. Now and then we will tell you about one. You will not be under a formal obligation. But you will be favorably disposed toward our recommendations and will give them a careful hearing. Is that fair? Does everyone consider that fair?"

Solly was nodding. Shy's smile was powered by loving warmth. Billy gave me a thumbs up.

I was also glad to see Robby's amusement. "I must say, Mr. Buckman, that you'd have made a hell of a businessman! Still, I would rather cut a deal with you than the ghost of Aleister Crowley."

"And you'll walk up those stairs with us?"

"I wouldn't do it alone. But with you at my side? Yeah. I'll check out those locked rooms in Daddy's castle. I can't keep running from this. The evil partner got passed on to me, and I have to settle my estate. I also want to say I'm sorry Summers ever hired that idiot Drivell. It was entirely his idea, and I signed on without giving it much thought. I think now that I'll have my programmers at Fantasy Fantasy concoct a serious ghost hunter. Maybe someone like you, Mike. He could prove to be a popular character. However. I hope you won't mind if I move to a hotel in Oxnard?"

"Sensible thing to do," I replied. "I was going to suggest it myself. I'll be curious to know whether the dreams stop or become less imperative."

We shook hands. I sent Robby back to the mansion to call Wagner Summers, explain the situation, and request him to deliver the keys and any other pieces of the estate still in his possession as soon as possible.

"This letter," I said, now alone with the Ghost Killers, "means that the third floor of the Sarka turret could potentially transform the history of occultism. Benedek acts like a handsomely compensated employee. He served the Crowley spirit. But in another way, old Sarka had plenty to crow about. What a triumph! He had trapped the ghost of the modern world's most feared and respected black magician. He literally captured Crowley on film! Surely that must be counted among the great prizes of the occult world.

"But of course a dangerous one. The ghost co-opted the life of his captor." I looked around at the team. Cheyenne sent me, in her quiet nod, a secret sign of approval. "This Crowley ghost is not one that any of us would want to have running loose in the world. Perhaps his main innovation as a magician was to fuse more thoroughly than before Buddhist sexual practices with the traditional Luciferian goals of western black magic. He studied eastern body disciplines, reaching the *Dhyāna* level in Yoga meditation. Elaborating and expanding eastern techniques, Crowley devised the rites and rituals prescribed in the VII° through the XI° degree in the OTO scheme of esoteric knowledge. Throughout his life he enjoyed initiating acolytes into the system. In London in 1942, the young Benedek Sarka must have been among the last students to enjoy the magus's hands-on attentions. He later, you may remember from that Kerrigan piece in *Video Watchdog*, made an underground film called *Seventh Degree*. Crowley probably masturbated the boy in some fashion. His formal sex magic begins with masturbation in the lower degrees, moves on to heterosexual rites, and concludes in the highest rungs with homosexual explorations. Crowley did a lot of all three, but openly preferred the homosexual area. That may help you to understand your current dream lives. His 'Sending' or whatever it is means to find out how well we perform through the entire system.

"The Crowley ghost bargained for Benedek's sexual life. You have to think your way into this. What would ghosthood mean to a spirit like Crowley? He had no body, and that must have terrified him. He was still fettered to place. He was in fact attached to a vulnerable strip of transparent plastic with a gelatin emulsion on one side. It could be burned or cut or disfigured in numerous ways. But no body and therefore no sexual capacity. No more ingesting drugs to transform his consciousness. No sex power from his fancy rites and practices to transform into magical will. He needed Sarka as, in effect, a substitute body. The Crowley ghost must have devised some vampire-like way of feeding on the energy from Sarka's sexual labors. Along these lines, one has to grant that Old Crow's naming of Benedek during their initial meeting in London did indeed have a divining force. The overriding duty of Sarka's whole life from that moment on was to serve as Crowley's body or Sanctissimus Carnem.

"Another of this man's major innovations in the field of black magic was his renewal of the disgraced Elizabethan tradition of John Dee and Edward Kelley. There is a lot of textual corruption in this material. Dee was a respected wizard recognized as such by the Queen. Kelley was almost certainly a low-minded con man. Since their day, many practicing magicians have feared having anything to do with the Dee/Kelley "Enochian magic," which is a standard name for angel conjuring. Paul Foster Case, who ran a mystical lodge in Los Angeles called the Temple of Adytum, thought that trying to bind angels and demons endangered the health of a magician. These practices, Case believed, had cut short the life of his friend Michael Whitty. Whitty had become acquainted with this magic as a member of the Order of the Golden Dawn, to which Crowley also belonged before shifting his energies to the OTO. Crowley reported stunning successes in the Enochian tradition."

Solly broke in. "Why does old Sarka call this Crowley dude 'Baphomet'? Is that an angel name?"

"It's for sure an ugly name," Shy remarked. "Rhymes with 'vomit.'"

I knew about Baphomet, and Shy was right: the rhyme pointed the way. This guy did indeed reside on the ugly side of the spectrum. "Crowley relates Baphomet to Mithras in the Roman mystery cult. Sometimes Baphomet is a subsidiary prince of Hell, or *Put Satanachia*, the Sabbath Goat. In this guise he is said to be the supreme general of Hell's army. This is the just the kind of demon that an Enochian practitioner would desire to conjure. Supposedly, a skillful black magician can conjure these creatures without worshipping them, and bargain with them for the use of their powers."

Solly had a further question. "How many kinds of angels are there, anyway? One bunch loyal to God and another sworn to Satan? One group of nice angels, one group of demons?"

"I'm just a researcher, Solly. I've never seen an angel and I'm not sure I would want to."

Shy spoke to his question. "There are lots of angel traditions. Sometimes one hears of neutral angels. Conscientious objectors, so to speak. They didn't swear loyalty to God or Satan. Then there's that passage in Genesis about the 'sons of God' (fallen angels, presumably) mating with human beings and producing a race of giants, all of whom perished in the Flood. If you assume angels could take human forms of either gender, these fallen angels both mothered and fathered, generating a breed of hybrid creatures, part human and part angelic. Perhaps, when they died, most or all of them went to Hell. Spirits of this hybrid type also appear in black magic."

Listening to her, I thought back to my conversation with Kerrigan and his emphasis on Crowley's love for Milton. *Paradise Lost* must have seemed to this man a sublimely poetic conjurer's manual.

I continued with the subject of his Enochian works. "Crowley claimed to have contacted his own guardian angel, Aiwass, who dictated to him the fundamentals of a new religion called Thelema.

"Founding a religion is a mark of high distinction in black magic because this labor causes others to lose or change their faith. So that was another feather in his cap. In more conventional realms, he edited grimoires and ancient treatises, wrote long commentaries on numerous magical texts and practices. He published poems, stories, novels, plays, memoirs, journals, autobiographies, self-help manuals, philosophical speculations. Yesterday I called the academic who wrote that Sarka piece I read you in the car, a guy named Kerrigan, and he told me that there wasn't much in the world of magic, much in the world period, that Crowley did not try to make his own. As he once put it, 'I never outgrew the feeling that the universe was mine to suck.'

"The man now enjoys considerable fame and cultural prestige. I'm sure the Crowley spirit knows that. He is the dark prince of rock 'n roll. His picture appears on the cover of *Dr. Pepper's Lonely Heart Club Band*. For a time he preoccupied Mick Jagger. Remember *Sympathy for the Devil*? 'Every cop's a criminal, and all the sinners saints.' It isn't so much the cops being criminals. It's the sinners being saints. That's a Crowleyan senti-ment for sure. Jimmy Page of Led Zeppelin amassed a vast private collection of Crowley man-uscripts, and for some years owned Boleskine, the Scottish estate where Laird Crowley performed magical experiments. David Bowie fooled around with his ideas. You'll find Crowley in Iron Maid-en, Daryl Hall, David Tibet, Curt Cobain, and

Marilyn Manson, of course, that blend of Monroe and Charlie. Take a listen to Lady Gaga's *Judas*. There's Crowley in there too.

"So that, briefly, is the man whose ghost we'll be meeting in a few minutes on the third floor of Sarka's turret. Maybe he's never managed to control his sexual 'transfers,' as Benedek called them. But I suspect Crowley has put some sexual whammy on us to test how well we could do the job Benedek had. We seem to have potential. As I said when Robby was here, I've noticed that sexual thoughts from my dreams are leaching into my everyday consciousness. Am I alone?"

Everyone looked glum and ashamed. Heads nodded.

"We better try to think ahead. Like his master Satan, Crowley will want to close us in the jaws of a binding contract. His last servant was a world-class performer of the Faust story.

"Possibly we could refuse the deal and survive. We might be able to flee the vicinity of the ghost. He is somehow fused with a film print. His sphere of magical influence might be severely limited. On the other hand, Benedek indicates in his letter that the Crowley ghost has become stronger and more active in the course of his lifetime. We might not be able to escape."

Billy stirred, telling me with his gestures that he wanted to speak. I was glad of that, since I myself was winding down toward a discouraging finish.

"OK," he began. "Say we forgot the million dollar payoffs and the inside track on charity donations. Say we washed our hands of this business. We would still be leaving a mess around that someone, for the good of humanity, will one day have to clean up. Much the simplest, cleanest outcome is for us to do the job right now. That's going to require an unimaginable act of cunning or a jackpot of good luck or both. We don't practice magic. We have little chance of casting a spell sturdy enough to impede or imprison this ghost magus.

"But knowledge is power, as the saying goes. Mike's been leading by example. The best thing to do is learn all we can about the Crowley ghost."

Robby called a half hour later. He had the keys.

CHAPTER SIX

Robby put a key into the privacy lock, and turned it. There was a solid thwock as the deadbolt disengaged. He inserted another key into the lock beneath the knob. This time the turn produced a sweet oiled click. The opened door swung back silently on its steel hinges. I had expected creaking.

As Marta held back, watching us with a sullen stare, The Ghost Killers followed Robby into the bottom landing of a staircase. Stained glass windows in ornamental shapes provided illumination for the entire area. To the right was another door. Robby did the honors again. Though we knew from Marta that the bottom floor chamber had served as Benedict's office, we wanted to see it.

The desk was massive. I sensed that the piece had been made within the last fifty years, but the style and craftsmanship harkened back to the Elizabethan period. On oak shelves was a quite large collection of books by and about Christopher Marlowe. I judged there to be around a thousand volumes. Other shelves held much smaller collections of English authors and politicians of Marlowe's day, various classical and continental works, and the history of the English stage, including costuming. There was a half bath with a sink.

Robby, Solly, and I lined up and used it.

We climbed the stairs to the second floor. Its room could best be described as a magical sex playground. There were upholstered tables and lavish thrones and a quilted leather bed. At the center of one wall a cushioned black altar squatted. It looked as if it had hosted lurid acts. On the floor was a deep blue carpet woven with various with magical sigils. There was also a lavish bathroom on this floor.

Two enormous mirrors faced each other across the room. They were, I suppose, a nod to the aristocratic rake's classic vices of exhibitionism and voyeurism. In this setting you could, like a camera, see what you were doing. Bianca Zitnik had not mentioned a room devoted to sexual adventure, but I felt sure that this was the setting her stories had implied.

I knew what to expect in the highest room. We were ascending through the hierarchy of Benedek Sarka's obsessions. On the bottom was Marlowe, the theater, and his career. Sexuality stood above that. The final room, surely, would be devoted to his spiritual aspirations.

It was indeed the black magician's den. This, clearly, was where the magical works were conceived and the spells cast. There were more oak bookshelves. These housed the hundreds of books and journals by Aleister Crowley published during and after his life, books on Crowley or with chapters on Crowley, magical guides and treatises, grimoires, etc. A black marble floor had three inlays forming three gold pentagrams inscribed in three white circles. At the north end of the room was a movie projector and a line of comfortable leather chairs. At the south end a screen awaited the projector's image. To the west, windows looked upon the coastline below, where one could view the moon's ancient and still turbulent love affair with the sea's edge. From this height I could barely make out the tiny hordes of sand crabs washed ashore in the waves, at home in water as well as air.

Another huge mirror, ornately framed, hung in this room. It retained second-floor associations with exhibiting and beholding. The projector and screen assured the continued evocation of a sexual atmosphere. But this mirror stood more generally for magic itself. Sorcery had always been done with mirrors, in the presence of mirrors. The air held odors from burnt stems and leaves. Seeking the origin of these smells led my eyes to an altar, higher than the one in the sex playroom. A wide obsidian bowl rested on it. Smoke, too, had always been the close associate of magic. It dissolved upwards, seeming to pass from earth to the

134

heavens and stars surrounding us. Smoke and mirrors. Lucifer, the bringer of light, was celebrated here.

"I imagine you know how to run a film projector," Billy said to me.

"Yeah."

"You better look over that one. There seems to be a film in it, ready to go."

The machine was a 16mm Bell & Howell 1500 sound projector refitted with a halogen bulb. A film had already been prepared for viewing. I had no doubt that it was Benedek Sarka's movie of the death of Aleister Crowley. He had probably threaded the film into the projector at some time shortly before his death.

The projector chosen implied that the film had been shot in sound. That surprised me. But of course, I told myself, equipment and lab fees meant nothing to the young Sarka. The budgets for his home movie experiments had no limit.

The threading had been properly done. The sprockets were in the sprocket holes. The feed spool turned smoothly. The film's leader was already attached to the take-up spool. I ran the machine for a few frames. The bulb was strong. The tilt controls had the picture at the right height.

"The projector is loaded," I announced. "Just close the curtain on the ocean view and turn out the lights when you're ready."

"Do you think the ghost will pop out of the projector?" Solly asked.

I shrugged. "Could be. Would you like to sit closer to the screen?"

No one, including me, found humor in my small joke. Billy shut the curtains. The five of us settled down in a line behind the projector, turning on two table lamps in that part of the room. I toggled the start switch. The machine rattled gently.

There were no titles. It just began.

We beheld a door marked with the number 13. The door opened. The camera moved into a small, seedy, sparsely furnished room. We heard nothing at first but the low crackling hum of a live mike. I assumed that, as Benedek Sarka had written, this was a room in Netherworld, the rooming house in Hastings where Crowley had died on Dec. 1, 1946.

The camera slowly panned a wall lined with Crowley's own disturbing art, clearly inspired by the devil. There was a self-portrait of a hairless figure with a long tapering chin and tiny rosebud mouth, wearing a placard around his neck on which was written TO MEGA THERION 666 (The Beast 666). Another depicted a totem pole whose main figure had horns and ugly teeth. Behind the pole other faces grimaced and grinned. Demons were everywhere.

We panned past a chimney crammed with books. Then we saw a curtained window, before which was a chair loaded with coats and a table bearing piles of books, a pitcher, and two glasses. The camera moved on to record another wall of demon drawings, several chairs, then a door, then finally a bed on which a thin figure lay beneath the covers, propped up against a bank of pillows and staring at the camera. On his bedside table was, not an electric lamp, but a heavy and ornate silver candelabra. Five candles were lit. The camera approached him. We heard the wheeze and rasp of his breathing. He was obviously deathly ill, and only his face was exposed, but it was Crowley, all right. The young piece of Sanctissimus Carnem from America, heir to Sarka Steel International, had come to film his passing.

Suddenly the configuration of the image shifted drastically. The conventional rectangle disappeared, and in its place was a pentangle. All the space outside the five-spoked figure was as black as night. In terms of the scene being recorded, only seconds appeared to have elapsed. Inside the mystical symbol was the same man on the same bed. I surmised that the camera operator, no doubt young Benedek Sarka, had merely paused for a moment to change to this novel lens.

Kerrigan said in *Video Watchdog* that Sarka had experimented with new designs for movie cameras. One of them, the one used to shoot this footage, must have been an occult movie camera with a unique set of lenses. Besides the usual array of varying focal lengths, this lens wheel also had a pentagonal option. In terms of the projection frame, the occult lens produced a pentagram of motion picture inscribed within a rectangle of darkness. In terms of the camera lens, however, it was a pentagram inscribed within a circle, the ancient symbol of magical power. The doorknob downstairs that had to be turned before we could enter this tower bore that symbol. On the floor of this screening room were three pentagrams-in-circles. You could achieve almost the same effect by masking off a star shape in an ordinary round camera lens. But I didn't think the area surrounding such a pentangle in the resulting film would be as black as it was in this movie unless the lens had actually been ground to that shape.

"I'm Aleister Crowley," the man within the star said in a cultured British accent. "You will soon be witnesses to my death."

The scene shifted. We were still in the same room. But a middle-aged woman was there, giving Crowley an injection (I supposed it was one of his daily heroin shots, having read that his doctor had at the end agreed to a *per diem* dose of eleven grams). She chatted with the dying mage about the forecast. Hearing of rough weather to come, Crowley shook his head and remarked, "This isn't a bad world to be leaving." At his suggestion she opened the window a mite. Then a man, thin and mustached, supervised Crowley's signing of several documents. Crowley instructed him, after his death, to be sure to take his watch.

Then a young man with an American accent visited with Crowley. They reminisced briefly about The Order of the Golden Dawn and Crowley's feud with the Irish poet William Butler Yeats. I thought the young American might be a literary scholar named Richard Ellmann, who was studying at the University of Dublin in 1946 while researching his biography of Yeats. This young man, I had read, visited Netherworld during the magus's last days.

A man with wavy hair and a toothbrush moustache appeared in the room. Crowley spoke German with him. He had to be the film actor Frederic Mellinger. The end was near. I remembered that Mellinger had visited on the last day of Crowley's life.

Time jumped forward again. The woman who had earlier injected Crowley and the thin man who was to take his watch were present in the room. The woman, visibly flustered, left the camera's pentangle. The man sat on the edge of the bed, and Crowley grasped his shoulders. The magician made a remark. Then he convulsed, subsided briefly, and convulsed again, screaming and thrashing. The camera moved closer, placing the center of Crowley's face at the center of its star lens. He fell back on the pillows with his eyes and mouth open. The camera stared at him. A woman's hand appeared in the pentagram holding a mirror. She placed it against Crowley's mouth. "No need for that," the man declared. "He's gone."

Crowley's remark had been distinct and clear. I won't soon forget it. His last words were "Sometimes I hate myself."

A loud crack erupted on the soundtrack. The camera turned quickly toward the window, in time to record a gust of wind from its open half inch fluttering the linen and riffling the pages of an open book on the nearby table.

Off camera the woman said, "The gods are greeting him."

The film ended. Its tail entered the projector. The screen brightened.

At the exact moment the film ended a form materialized out of or just in front of the screen, then stepped aside. He wore a black robe embroidered with stars and astrological designs, and appeared younger than he had been at his death.

"Do what thou wilt shall be the whole of the law," he solemnly intoned, as if quoting scripture.

He broke into an ironic smile. "Please allow me to introduce myself. I'm Aleister Crowley. You are now witnesses to my rebirth."

Hip to Mick Jagger! The Crowley spirit had become acquainted with his posthumous career in western culture. Vanity is one sin that does not require a body.

"I hope to become the partner of each and every one of you. We should keep this simple, don't you think? Full context would just weigh us down and slow us down. Have you noticed that? That the complexities never really matter?

"You have within you elements that are yours alone and cannot be taken away. One such element is the power and sense of well-being you derive from sex in all its forms. You have access to ecstasy. Euphoria is not beyond your grasp. You derive so many benefits from that knowledge! It proves that, despite the hardness of life, you still have the best things around. I need this well-being. My magic needs it. My project of self-fulfillment needs it. And I can have it *if* you consent. Once I have your permission, I can take it from there. I won't remove much from you. You thrive on this power. I'll take just enough that your sexual desire will be somewhat increased. You'll want, as it were, to make up for the loss of the energies I have consumed.

"What can I give you in return? My knowledge. I could reveal the secrets of astral travel, of conjuring demons and angels, of the gnostic rites of Lucifer. The Twelfth Degree of magic attainment is mine alone. To finish earning it in 1924, I had to die spiritually in all four of the elements. The last of these ordeals was my death in the Sphere of Fire. I returned to my perished body and person, but from then on I have been a god, and have taken the title due me, *Ipsissimus*, most supremely myself. With my guidance, all spiritual attainments could be within your grasp.

"You would of course be given the complete map of my sexual knowledge. Its spaces are legion. You'll touch all the bases in that field. You'll know every rapture, for my sexual interests will interact with your real and private sexual desires. The result may be more of you than of me. It will be some form of collaboration, where you have the veto power, and satisfy your own true will. I can also assure that the people you deem sexually intriguing will be responsive to your lure. I am very good at romantic entrancement. Magicians have done distinguished work in this area for centuries, and I have built on their foundations. I can also give you a long and disease-free life. You'll die knowing you have seen it all. Dying always involves regrets. But yours will be minimal.

"That's the positive side of it. What of threats and punishments? Unlike the Faust stories, bargaining with me will not bring you eternal damnation. There is no damnation. Mr. Sarka served me well. He is now dead. But he led a fulfilling life and he is not writhing in Hell right now. Lucifer has more important things to do. You'll fare better than all but a few of the Fausts of literature, theatre, and screen. So *that* penalty is out of the picture.

"What can I impose on you should you choose not to cooperate with me? A lot, my dears. I did not require this area of magic when dealing with the sainted Benedek Sarka. One day I will put his statues in churches. He wondered in his letter to you, Robby, whether I could cause cancer?" The Crowley ghost strode over to young Sarka, who was sweating and visibly uncomfortable.

I observed the mirror behind him. The Crowley apparition was no movie vampire. He reflected. But his reflection jittered and flickered slightly like the bad print of a film.

"I *can* do that. I'm afraid I know all the plague spells. I can make your life a hell. Would I? Do I threaten that?" The ghost's blank stare bore into Robby. "Oh yes. I most certainly threaten that, though I firmly believe my proposal to be desirable on its own merits." Finished with Robby Sarka for the moment, the ghost moved to the front of the room.

He seemed to be gathering himself into a calm concentration. "No one ever deals with a magician without demanding a proof of his powers. It think of it as the Satanic version of doubting Thomas. Basically, you give a magician one try. If he attempts to display his wares and fails to convince, a second chance is rarely afforded him. I accept these terms.

"I am going to bring into this room a rather dispiriting chap named Choronzon. The name is perhaps Assyrian, perhaps earlier. I first brought him forth when wandering in the Sahara desert. I thought him the most loathsome creature imaginable. He seemed to me the metaphysical opposite of magic. Gradually I have come to find him amusing. I believe that, when performing a 'one chance trial,' this is the fellow who will do the trick. But what does it matter? Nothing matters."

He moved to the altar. "And so to work." He

took a handful of something from a pocket in his robe and threw it into the black bowl. He lit a match, and with the match a tinder, and with the tinder put flame to the stuff in the black bowl. Acrid fumes soon filled the room.

The Crowley ghost began an incantation. "I send to ZAX, the Tenth Aethyr. I seek demon 333 in the abyss between man and God. I call the Father of Dispersion, the Death of the Ego, to my presence. I call the opposite of all magic. Let your horror be here with us! Bring catastrophe on." He switched to Latin. I followed along well enough to know that he was repeating with elaborations what he had already said in English. From his tone, which was less stentorian and more reverential, I gathered that the English beginning had been a concession to our ignorance. He wanted us to appreciate his power. But Latin was actually doing the work. Demons preferred Latin, I supposed, because once they had learned to obey it.

Crowley started rhyming and playing around with kindred sounds. It reminded me of scat singing. "Zazaz, Zazas, Nastanda, Zasas, Zazaz, Zasa, Saza. . . ." There followed a long minute of this sassafras and razzmatazz.

I had read about Crowley's dealings with this particular demon. Choronzon had been difficult to control. The Magus had brandished his hand-forged magician's dagger to keep Choronzon at bay inside his circle. Crowley had loathed the damned thing. Today he had chosen, in other words, to repeat a shameful act of conjuring, and to show us an abhorrent creature inhabiting the abyss between man and God. This demonstration would again put on display, as his sexual Sending had, Crowley's compulsion to exhibit his own shames.

Being shameless sounded like a good thing when imagined abstractly. But the more I saw of this strenuous shamelessness, the more respect I felt for good old shame, the real thing, the kind you kept to yourself.

From within his robe Crowley extracted a silver cross. I believe the figure was known as a Calgary cross. There were three steps at its base. In Sunday school, we had been told that the steps represented Faith, Hope, and Charity. Crowley held the cross in his left hand. It was turned upside down, so that the stairs at the top led downwards. The Magus made the sign of the cross backwards, touching his two shoulders before his forehead and chest.

I heard a garble of low angry sounds. I was certain that the cacophony was composed of obscenities, but the phonemes were so overlapped and intermingled that nothing intelligible could be made out.

A creature appeared in the room, inside the southernmost of the great pentangles on the floor. Fetid odors accompanied him, things familiar from a human bathroom and some not familiar, drawn perhaps from a vault of unearthly cosmic stinks. It was humanoid, though with an oversized head, and naked. It wore a short black skirt. I couldn't tell its sex, since the breasts could be read as male or female. Its flesh was slightly bluish. It sat comfortably inside the pentagram inside the circle, its upper body resting on its feet and ankles. I recognized the position from my YMCA yoga class. Choronzon appeared in the pose known as The Thunderbolt.

It was a face to die of. At least mood swings had some sort of sense and structure. One was elated, then one was depressed. This was way beyond mood swings. On the internet yesterday I had stumbled onto a reference to figures named Chaos and Discord in John Milton's *Paradise Lost*. The poet described Chaos as having a "visage incomposed" and Discord as having "a thousand various mouths." Something of that order was now in the room. One facial expression became another, became another, in a slow tumbling rhythm. He was abject. He was obsequious. He was conniving. He was baleful, meddlesome, surprised, rapturous, gaping, alarmed, nervous, dumb, mad, determined, angry, lascivious, frivolous, confused, flirtatious, suspicious, triumphant, defiant, devil-may-care, expressionless, and on and on through look after look.

What did any of them matter? Choronzon's was the face of Chaos and Discord. Here was pure-form futility. Being this and then that, the demon was none, null, nothing. I was falling into a whirl-pool of nausea. The face kept tumbling from attitude to attitude, and this unceasing self-cancellation seemed to suck in everything. Creation was undone. Crowley had said that Choronzon was the metaphysical opposite of magic. Magic, for Crowley, was the transformation of reality into the image of the magician's will. No will here, no creation here. No Crowley in Choronzon, no me, no anybody. Just a primordial indifference of eternal willy-nilly. I was very close to vomiting. I tried looking away from Choronzon, but the whole room, all of reality, was flickering like an old movie image. Nonbeing, chew by chew, was eating Being.

Out of the corner of my eye I saw Solly rise to his feet and raise the chair he had been sitting in above his head. He made a run toward Choronzon. "I can't stand you! You shouldn't be!"

Suddenly Crowley stood between Solly and the

insufferable demon. "Stop! Stop this second!"

Solly stopped, his body throbbing with rage. The chair started forward twice. But his control remained in force. He put the chair down.

He should have slammed that chair into Choronzon's horrible face, but he hadn't! Maybe I should try using the projector. Indifferent to our distress, the demon kept demonstrating his nullity. My mind reeled. I was slipping into madness.

"Cease, Choronzon! Return your horribleness to the Tenth Aethyr." There was another bout of rhyming and sound play. Crowley made another backwards sign of the cross, this time using a dagger. The creature disappeared.

"That will, I trust, be a motive to bargain. How would you like a month of Choronzon dreams? You really should hear him speak. He has a most rousing monologue where he vows to raid the throne of God, bite off his penis, chew it up and spit it into the abyss. It has quite an effect on auditors.

"Much the best course, as Benedek wrote, is to make a pact with me. What does Trump call it? The art of the deal, I believe. Think over your situation. A week should be sufficient. You are all expected here next Wednesday."

"I have a question," Shy asked.

Crowley smiled. "And what is that?"

"You need our sexual energy for some magical work that will 'complete your self-fulfillment?' What work? What are trying to do?"

Crowley nodded. "I appreciate your interest in me. You are a most attractive woman, Mrs. Buckman. I have not had a Scarlet Woman of my own, or one really worth the name, since long before my death. I have little appeal to women who despise and mistrust men. For those traditional self-sacrificial women who seek to gratify men, and give them the ecstasies they seek, I hold great appeal. You, as I know from your dreams, are one of those. I will treasure your gifts.

"As for my goals, they have not wavered. I wish, as I did in my natural life, to forward the career of Lucifer in the world. He is not the twisted, hateful creature that Christian prejudice has promulgated. Nor am I the filthy beast of a John the Baptist that the very same prejudice has fashioned and condemned.

"I will be the first ghost to have returned, fully and unmistakably. How pathetic Houdini was, a stage magician from beginning to end! He couldn't even manage to get a message from Beyond to his beloved wife. Do you know of any ghosts who make appearances on the Sunday talk shows? Stay in the White House? Journey to trouble spots in the world to consult with political and spiritual leaders? Give interviews to major journalists? Appear at rock concerts? I will be the first truly to return. Do you doubt that people will hang on my every word?"

Shy was not about to flatter this twisted ambition. "You're just a ghost. You haven't come back from the dead. You're not alive. You haven't been resurrected."

Crowley again flashed his ironic smile. "You must be speaking of that other fellow purported to have come back, but centuries ago and only for a measly forty days. His return is the gold standard? The world, or rather the tiny portion of it to which he appeared, hardly had a chance in that short period to ask its first wave of questions. Do you really think the differences between him and me, assuming there really are any, will matter? I'll be back from death. The issue of whether or not I am resurrected will soon be regarded as a belated case of scholastic hair-splitting.

"I expect to do better than Jesus. I will be the one who returned forever and for all time. I won't abandon this life in three days, three years, or three centuries. I will answer all questions, provide unprecedented access. I will appear at the United Nations. I will appear in forsaken neighborhoods, at rallies, religious gatherings, sporting events. I will confer with the political, spiritual, artistic, scientific, academic, and military leaders of the world, address massive audiences, record interviews with journalists of all stripes. Historically, I have always held out a strong appeal to men. And as I have said, I will also attract women who love to fulfill men. Who knows? The Risen, they may call me, the light of a new dawn. I'm not a conqueror or a brainwasher. I will by the sheer power of my existence establish my religion. 'Love is the law, love under will,' I preached during my lifetime."

Shy wasn't finished, however. I found myself wishing for the first time that her courageous tongue would be ruled by prudence and keep quiet.

"Your final judgment on your life was 'Sometimes I hate myself.' Do you really think the world will flock down a path leading to *that*?!"

Crowley stared down at her with amused contempt. "There is no final judgment. I'm back in this world and still speaking. Your assessment of human beings is insufferably naive. Who among you does not at some level and to some degree hate themselves? If you didn't, you would be stupider than you are. Will the multitude recoil from those words? Of course not. They will seem human, all too human, and will endear me to most.

"I see now that during my lifetime I was too biblical, too attached to the forms and pieties I was endeavoring to replace. This second time around the world will see a jauntier Crowley. I won't just throw truth in the face of my audience. No, I'll help them to follow me. I'll speak like this: 'I'm saying that you ought to do whatever the heck you want. No, make that whatever the *hell* you want. Why not? Just do it. Anything goes. Nothing is true. Tune in, turn on, drop out. It finally doesn't matter whether you succeed or whether you fail. Nothing matters except this. You really have to will what you want to do.' That's a positive message, is it not? After several months of a worldwide media blitz with me talking to the Big Cheeses and dominating them like a born spiritual trainer, I'll be the most influential figure in the world. My every sentence will set a trend or end a practice. My idle opinions will make or break giant corporations, perhaps entire nations.

"I will trumpet a new god for a renewed world. He is phallic, he is solar, he is liberating. Do what you want to do, no more and no less. Nothing matters. Everything is permitted. Every man and every woman is a star! There will be changes as Lucifer rises. Light will prevail. There will be no boundary between the text and the page! No spaces between the stars! There will be light!

Terrifying, revealing, and exciting light!"

Thankfully, he seemed to have come to the end. Perhaps he realized that he was getting close to Full Windbag Mode. Christians had always preached. I supposed it made sense that their inversion would preach too.

Crowley ordered me to rewind the film. On a shelf behind me was a film can and a steel strong box. I was to put the film in the can, and the can in the box.

"Do you want me to lock it?" I asked. I hadn't intended the deep sarcasm in my tone. But there it was, like the default mode in a computer. "Stow it on top of a tower and then double lock its quebracho wood door?"

The eyes bored into me. "Just do as I ask. Your sarcasm is tedious."

"So was your sermon."

I let it go at that and went about performing my appointed tasks. Everyone waited for me. As we walked out, shutting the door behind us, I was sandbagged by a violent headache. It got worse on the stairs. With every step that took me away from that high room, roots seemed to be ripping up from the earth of my mind. It hurt.

Let it hurt! I was glad to be leaving.

Cheyenne should have kept her mouth shut. Me too.

CHAPTER SEVEN

Robby and the Ghost Killers were gathered in the guest house living room. Marta had made us sandwiches, but no one was eating much. Robby, in particular, looked in a poor way. Besides his pallor, one eyebrow was twitching.

"I'll be leaving soon. To tell you the truth, I really did not expect to see a ghost today, whatever I said earlier. For years I have been trying to believe that my mother's talk about father's 'evil partner' referred to a psychological bent in him. I wasn't prepared at all for this Crowley ghost. The whole scene shocked me to the core. I want to go home for a while.

"I feel trapped in my father's world. One day I'm running my business and enjoying my life. The next I'm chained in the dungeon of my childhood."

"We don't yet know what to do, if indeed we can do anything," Billy said. "Could I have your home address and phone number?"

Robby took a business card out of his wallet and wrote down the information Billy requested.

"We'll be in touch when our plans have jelled," Billy assured him.

"Do you think I'll be safe at home?"

Billy looked down at the card he had just been handed. "In Newport? I don't think our apparition could actually visit you down in Orange County. In my experience ghosts are attached to a place. They have their haunts. This one seems bound to a film print. But think of that 'demonstration' or *demon*-stration we saw this morning. I'm not sure where the Tenth Aethyr is, but I suspect Choronzon doesn't reside anywhere close by. This ghost has the skills of a black magician. He can cast spells and address them to anyone anywhere.

"Sir James Frazier said that magic does its work through two main methods. It can take a likeness of someone or something, a doll, a picture, a statue, and try to change the someone or something by acting on the likeness. It can also work by the path of contagion or contiguity. The magician gets a hair or nail clipping or article of clothing, an object that has touched his target, and tries to change the target by acting on that object. When you left this house after graduating from high school did you leave toys behind? Clothes? All kinds of stuff?"

Robby nodded. "Of course I did. Come to think of it, I had a couple of magic sets with card tricks and simple vanishing illusions."

Billy threw up his hands. "Well, that's a vulnerability. Tell me, what do you think of Crowley's offer?"

"May as well ask us all," Solly said, "since the ghost is pitching us the same deal. I guess he figures that, the bigger his power pack, the more quickly he can become the world's most fascinating celebrity. It isn't fucking fair—that's one thing I think. If we were all children of old Mr. Sarka, then all right, the sins of the fathers and so on. But we're just employees doing a job. To be honest—"

"We can talk about this later, Solly," Billy intervened, trying to cut him off. "Right now we need to hear what Robby thinks."

But Solly was on a rampage, and wasn't about to be stifled. "Let me finish, for crying out loud. To be honest, it sounds like a pretty good deal. You get a long and disease-free life with lots of sex. Sounds nice. Who wouldn't want that? But the old bugger is going to be syphoning off your sexual satisfaction. I don't cotton to being that fucking fucker's hired fucker. Then again, I don't want to wake up with cancer or have that god-awful demon drop in for a nightcap. We're all trapped in Robby's cage, damn it to hell. "

"OK," Billy said. "Are you finished?" Solly nodded, red-faced and proud. "Again, what do *you* think, Robby?"

"I don't like the thought of my family curse lighting on you. It doesn't feel right to be paying anyone to take on the same drastic choice that I have to face. I was glad when your fees got raised this morning. But now the whole thought of employing you makes me feel cowardly and corrupt. If you leave me to face the choice alone, I'll understand. I don't think anyone, knowing the circumstances, would take your place."

Billy shrugged. "That's all very noble of you. I mean that. But it may well be a moot point. I doubt whether we can quit the situation just by terminating our agreement with you. As for your sense of cowardice and corruption. . . . We deal with ghosts. That's our business. That's the service we offer. If you are going to condemn yourself for hiring us, you might as well condemn us for going into business. This super-charged moral probity won't get you anywhere now. However the current situation came about, you're in it, and we're in it, like it or not.

"Mike pushed you on this point earlier today, and now I have to push you again. I want to know whether you think there is any chance that you may in the end do a deal with Crowley. Or are you dead set against that? That's the key issue, for you as well as for us. For one thing, it's possible Crowley would be content with you alone. He seems to have been gaining power and mobility under his pact with your father. For another thing, if you intend to strike a deal with Crowley and we plan some way of destroying him, then we would be working at cross-purposes, and you might well regret our efforts."

"Sorry, I hadn't seen that point. It's been a tough few days. But you're right, of course."

He paused. Billy waited, then pressed him again. "And?"

"My God, I don't know! It's not an easy choice, is it? When I think about everything involved, the attractions and the threats, the fact that he might be content with me alone and let you people off the hook, I can imagine, in the end, that might seem to me the best thing. But do I wish I had never met this Crowley ghost? Damn rights I do!"

"So. The outcome you would most prefer is his destruction or his impotence. That would amount to nearly the same thing as never having met him. He would be out of your life and out of ours."

"What if you fail, but the attempt enrages him?"

"That could happen," Billy said. "But I bet that he would not be so enraged as to destroy us all and leave himself wholly untended. Crowley is not yet so detached from the death documentary as he one day hopes to be. He won't do anything to spoil the possibility of that freedom. His main goal is to make a deal."

"Do you want anything else from me right now?"

"Haven't I been clear?" Billy said. "I want your permission to plot the death of this ghost."

"You have it, then," Robby replied, and rose to go. He seemed angry at having been forced into an unequivocal approval of a move against Crowley. At this stage, clearly, Robby wanted to be as free as possible. Should our attack fail, he would be forced to make a deal with Crowley. He was angry because, in that eventuality, he might have to pay dearly for our foolhardiness.

When Robby left, Billy discussed our immediate plans. We should also leave and drive home for a few days. It probably wouldn't make any difference so far as the dreams were concerned. The Sending had already turned into a receiving. But there was still the odd chance that its force might diminish if we were eighty miles away from the seething occult atmosphere of this estate. The main point of going home was to give us a chance to consider our course of action. That was better done in our normal surroundings, away from the demands and distractions of Folly's Cove.

This would be our last night in the guest house. Tomorrow morning we were returning to Santa Barbara County.

That evening I told Shy that I was going for a walk.

"Do you want company?" she asked me.

"Tell you the truth, I want some time alone to think over the events of the day."

"You go on off, then." She kissed me. "I'll be reading in the bedroom."

I didn't like fibbing to her, but she might otherwise have insisted on accompanying me. I wanted to do this by myself.

Approaching the main house, I could see a light in the living room. I heard faint voices followed by a gale of laughter. It was the soundtrack to a television sitcom. I knocked on the side door. The voices halted. Someone snapped on the porch light.

"It's you, Mike. Come on in," Marta said. "Can I get you anything?"

"No. I came over to talk to you."

She walked me into the yawning spaces of the living room, where the television had been left on mute. Marta used the remote to shut down her electronic hearth. I took the chair nearest her couch, and pulled it around until I was facing her.

"I want you to level with me. I think you know more about this house than you have let on."

"And why is that?"

"There was something in the way you eyed us as we entered the turret this morning, as if we were violating your space as well as your master's. You've lived alone here for twenty years with Benedek Sarka. I know the kind of man he was. He couldn't share a house with a good-natured, efficient, intelligent woman such as yourself without enjoying a long-standing affair with her. You know a great deal about this house, don't you?"

She was wearing a loose blue linen dress. Her hand emerged from a waist pocket holding a pack of cigarettes. She lit one and leaned back, mocking me in a mostly friendly way, her eyes sparkling and the ghost of a smile on her lips.

"Do you have any other suspicions?"

"As a matter of fact, I do. Crowley claims that he had a technique for inducing reciprocal desire in Sarka's sexual partners. I suspect that means that he placed some version of his sexual fantasy probe in your mind. Tell me, what is the long-term effect? Do you feel changed?"

"Changed? Heavens. Is there anything else?"

"A bit more, yes. Does the Crowley ghost come down at night and watch television with you?"

She took a drag. "What a thought! And where did that one come from?"

"Just this. The ghost has a fair grasp of the contemporary world—the prevalence of rock music, the role of media, and in particular the way media peddles and we buy into celebrity in all its varieties from infamy on up. He's been watching television. There aren't many televisions in the house. I suspect Benedek didn't care for the medium. This screen right here, the one you were watching when I knocked, is the one nearest the tower. The others are on the second story, which does not connect with the turret tower. I believe it is difficult for Mr. Crowley to move very far away from a certain can of film. I think he quite likely watches this screen. You also watch it. Ergo, you watch it together."

Her smirk had disappeared, replaced by a look of anxious intrigue. "If all that is so, this ghost will be listening to us at this very instant. He will know what I say to you."

"Or perhaps not. The time he spent with us today involved an immense expenditure of energy. Sarka has not served him in weeks. I think he may be exhausted for the time being."

"Mr. Buckman, let's go outside and sit on the patio. I can turn on a light out there if you prefer."

We went through French doors leading from the living room to the walled patio overlooking the sea. Lamplight spilling out of large windows filled this space with a pale glow. I didn't need more. But Marta wanted to sit all the way down at the corner of the house farthest away from the turret. I consented to a small spotlight meant only for the northern tip of the patio.

The night was heavy with moisture, nearly smothering the running lights of passing ships. Marta began her tale.

"You're right about the exhaustion. When I turned out the kitchen lights this evening, he appeared in the shadows and told me that he would not be down for television tonight."

Marta's involvement with Benedek Sarka began when her mother and father retired to Arizona. Benedek had been extremely generous to her mother, allowing her family to occupy the guest cottage. Her mother thought him an odd and secretive man, but had never warned her daughter to beware of lustful advances or indeed said anything indicating untoward behavior on his part.

Marta was not a sound sleeper. Her employer knew of her frequent restlessness, since the lights in her bedroom were often on throughout the night and her lighted window could be observed from the patio. Sarka was a poor sleeper himself, and often spent the wee hours sipping whisky on the patio. Late one night, as Marta sat in bed reading magazines, Sarka knocked on her bedroom door. Since neither of them were able to sleep, perhaps she would like to come down for a drink? She promised to join him in a few moments. After freshening up, changing into her most comely sleepwear, and donning her nicest robe, she joined him downstairs.

They wound up doing slightly kinky but entirely exciting things to each other in the turret's second-floor playground. It became a matter of routine. Whenever Sarka was in residence, the two would once a week enjoy a drink and a few toots of marijuana or both and wind up having fun together in the "Lust Palace" or "Hot Spot," two of Benedek's favorite nicknames for the room I have been calling the sex playground.

She had had some boyfriends, a few serious suitors. But these relationships had all fizzled out in the end. It was hard work finding the right sort of partner. She enjoyed the convenience, regularity, and lustful energy of the Sarka affair. Marta at that point in her life neither expected love and marriage, nor wanted them. The arrangement filled a void, but left her independence intact. In a way, her affair flattered the pride she had always felt in taking good care of the house.

She was not aware of any foreign invasion of her sexual fantasies. Her dreams today were versions of the dreams she had always had. Eventually Sarka told her that he had a "special relationship" with an eminent ghost who resided in his tower suite. It was important to this ghost, he said, that his life be happy and satisfied. Sarka would sometimes joke about their second-floor escapades. "Hex sex," he called it. Once he informed her that the ghost was particularly pleased with their relationship. "He tells me that you are a natural, a perfect partner. He would not wish you any different than you are. No modifications required. And I agree wholeheartedly!"

Sarka told her that the ghost would not haunt the house proper. He preferred to keep to himself in the tower. But five or six years ago the ghost began to manifest itself when Marta was alone in the living room watching television. To this day, she never saw the Crowley spirit coming in or out of rooms or gliding through open spaces. He preferred more dramatic manifestations. "I never see him moving continuously about the house. He likes to float out from dark corners and shadowy walls. It used to frighten me, but I have grown used to his peculiarities. Gods knows I have my own."

From the many dark spaces in that huge living room the ghost would slowly come into focus like a camera effect in an old haunted house movie. Marta had some bad scares. But she was a pragmatic woman. There was a ghost in her house. What did he want? She felt that, before materializing, the ghost seemed to have been lurking there, invisible, intent on the television. She noticed that he always materialized in a place from which the television screen could be viewed. He was watching too!

How could the ghost be made comfortable? The next time he appeared, she scooted over, making room for him on the couch. The ghost instantly disappeared. The next time, she again scooted over. But she smiled and patted the empty cushion next to her, moving her eyes from the ghost to the couch to the ghost. "Most gracious of you," Crowley said, and took a seat beside her. In nights to come, Marta showed him brief snatches of all the available programming. He preferred news-related shows, CNN and Fox especially, and talk shows. He would ask her questions about the guests, the people they mentioned, the events they referred to, the products being advertised. He had died, he told her, in 1946, and had a lot to learn.

"Did you tell Sarka about these cozy TV-watching sessions?"

"Yes," Marta replied, as if there were no reason in the world for her not to tell him. "Benny was amused. He said he had been wondering how his ghost had suddenly become so hip. I think he was pleased that the ghost and I had found a way of getting along. I thought I had freed him from a chore or duty. I hope that I did. Benny always seemed to me a little bit hurried, a little bit on edge, except when we were making love. Time never seemed an issue then. Nothing but pleasure mattered then."

"Has the ghost become more mobile in recent years?"

"Perhaps. One night he asked me about supermarkets, and I offered to drive him into town the next day and show him one. After all, a look at the real thing is worth a thousand pictures, as my father used to say. Well, that was a no-no! He refused in a huff. But for the last two or three years I have occasionally seen him in the shadows of the yard. I'm not sure whether he visits the beach, but once I thought I saw him lurking near those caves you explored. He seems more outgoing, more confident than he was when I first saw him in the living room."

What a housekeeper! Benedek Sarka had left her half a million dollars, and she was worth every penny of it.

We said goodnight. Marta returned to the house via the living room. I started walking back to the guest quarters. But I stopped on the dark edge of the patio and waited.

Out at sea lightning flickered. I heard the thunder drums. Warm rain began to fall.

The TV went back on. From my angle I could see through a picture window the backside of her couch and half the television screen in front of it. She switched to a news broadcast. I thought I recognized the anchor, an attractive woman who worked at CNN. There seemed to have been another urban shooting with racial overtones. A panel of talking heads were expressing heated opinions about the incident. I waited. The Crowley ghost, stark naked, appeared in a dark area left of the screen, and floated to the couch. He took a seat. I could not see him anymore, just the high back of the couch, so I began tiptoeing along the picture window toward the couch. Gradually the couple came into view.

A bolt of lightning spotlit the scene. Marta sat with her skirt hiked up, revealing frilly red panties. Crowley stared at them.

Then, by the glow of the lamplight and the TV screen, I watched his spirit body throb, swelling with desire and then sinking with frustration. It wasn't a real body, of course, but a manifestation generated by the ghost. Still, the visible Crowley was the most physical part of Crowley, and that wisp of embodiment was locked in a rhythm of frustration. Swell, collapse. Desire, denial. I was reminded of the games with delayed orgasm that Bianca had described. This looked like ceaseless delay, Tantalus rather than Tantras.

I stumbled on a table. Crowley's head whipped around to the window. Another bolt of lightning exposed us both. I saw fury in his eyes. But I also saw embarrassment. A voyeur had caught the old libertine in a shameful act.

I retreated into the shadows and jogged back to the cottage.

Shy put her book down. "It wasn't a walk, was it?"

Grabbing a towel from the bathroom, I explained the reason behind my fib. She wasn't buying.

"What are you protecting me from? There is danger here, obviously, and we have all been exposed to it. Why can't we interview Marta together?"

"I was afraid that Crowley would put in an appearance. He expressed a clear interest in you. When you showed him your fighting Christian spirit, I thought he was even *more* interested.

Defiling a Christian earns you extra credit where he comes from. As a matter of fact, I did see Crowley."

I told her of my visit to the mansion, leaving nothing out.

"What do you imagine was going on between Marta and Crowley?" she asked when I was finished.

"I'm not sure. Somehow, as we know, ghosts can see and hear. That much of the body has been left them. Maybe those two senses are enough to heighten Crowley's desire and lessen the pain of its thwarting? But I thought of Tantalus in the classical stories, his tongue so close to the water but doomed never to touch it."

Shy thought for a few moments. "When we get home, I'm going to talk to my mother about this case. Your Wilbur doesn't seem to be a sex-tormented ghost. But my mother's ghost was more like Crowley. He might have been worse than Crowley. Remember, he mentored a serial killer. She might have a useful perspective."

"You're right. I shouldn't have resisted that idea the first time you brought it up. I need to get out of these wet clothes and take a shower."

When I returned from the bathroom, I got under the covers. Shy turned to me. We snuggled. Then I ruined it. "I'm sorry, but there's something we have to talk about, Shy. Crowley said that you were the sort of woman who would respond positively to him and to his offer. Do you know what he meant?"

Cheyenne rolled over on her back, propped her pillow, and sat up. My doing, my fault. I had raised an issue at the wrong time. Damn.

"These dreams. I'm far from selfless, you know. I dream of my own sexual pleasure. But in the dreams I am aware that the source of all this sexual agitation is male. I must admit, I rather like that. Giving someone such a gift. . . . I think I'm a responder more than an initiator. What turns me on is satisfying you, Mike. I've always wanted a man to adore. And man, do I have one!"

I put my head in her lap.

"The sort of woman, in other words, that Crowley imagines he can attract."

Her answer was quick and sure. "Enter into that putrid partnership with him? Never. I already have everything I want." She began running her fingers through my hair. "His whole seduction depends on a Faust who thinks that something must be added to his life to make it complete and fulfilled. Something that God's creation has not supplied and therefore only Satan can deliver."

"Well," I said, filled with brimming joy, "I didn't expect to find a satanist buried in your soul."

"Don't be so sure. That phrase, 'the devil made me do it.' My mother used to say that often when I was a child. I started saying it too when I was little, and now and then I still say it. Would you like to play some more of those delayed orgasm games? Don't pretend that you haven't been dreaming and fantasizing about them. We all have. I suppose our Crowley dreams started that way because delayed orgasm is the lowest rung of his sexual magic. What would that be? VII°? Whatever. Sometimes the complexities really *don't* matter. I've been thinking up some truly devastating ways of teasing you, Mike. I wouldn't be surprised to see tears. Along those lines, I wouldn't mind hearing some convincing begging. But I have a cold cold heart, and you mustn't expect mercy to come easily. I'm sure the devil is making me do this. Why don't you take off those boxer shorts?"

Boy I did. Boy did I.

CHAPTER EIGHT

It had been such an anxious trip that the first sight of our home, still nestled among Central California's sun-browned and oak-dotted hills, exactly as we had left it, was unusually fortifying.

But of course things were not as we had left them. The place was a mess. During our four nights in Ventura, I had forgotten all about the construction project begun three days ago and still at the stage of wanton and enthusiastic demolition. Workers in masks armed with crowbars and sledge hammers roamed the house's formerly placid spaces. I tried not to dwell on the rubble in the kitchen, the missing wall between the kitchen and the family room, the old cabinetry half extracted from the hall bathroom, the clouds of dust and plaster in the air. Cheyenne and I got to the bedroom, where each of us filled a suitcase with clean clothes. A quick chat with Ben and Valentina, and we were off to our rental in New Aarhus.

Cheyenne had made a shopping date with her mother, who soon pulled into our new driveway. While the two of them were at the supermarket tracking down everything from laundry supplies and sundries to food and drink, I sat under the rental's covered back porch, looking at browning lawn and two sorry beeches as I spoke with my taciturn boarder.

"Wilbur?"

"Mike."

"You must understand, Grandad, that we have to derail Crowley. I've never asked you about ghosts, but I will now. For years Valentina was possessed by the ghost of her grandfather. You have lived in my mind for over half my life. But I don't think that all ghosts learn how to enter the mind of a living person. Is that right?"

"Yes. The trick is normally learned from another ghost. But you're right, few ghosts know it."

"Who taught it to you?"

"I met a ghost in my graveyard in Paso Robles. He was passing a quiet day while his host, his oldest son, was playing golf. Said he couldn't stand to be in his son's mind while he was wrapped up in that crazy game. The brief flares of joy, the spurts of angry and obscene self-deprecation, and above all the abiding undercurrent of hopelessness were more than he could bear. He showed me the way."

"Is it hard to do?"

"Not to get in. Getting out, however, takes some practice."

"That's good news. We can use that to put a scare into Crowley."

"Do I figure in this plan?"

"It's just a sketch at this point, but yes, you figure. Could you reconsider the possibility of visiting Valentina? When I asked you about it, you had sensed a romantic angle to her long years of hosting her grandfather. You didn't want to mislead her. You feared that she would be all too eager to please you in ways that had once pleased her grandfather. Well, you were right about the romantic angle. But this is an emergency, grandad. You need to partner with Valentina."

"Crowley is a menacing ghost. And that headache spell he put on you hurt me as well. Took a long while before I felt myself again. Yes, Mike. I'll help in any way I can."

"Great! Thank you! For this to work, you and Valentina will have to function as a team. We only have a few days. I think you should spend as much time inside her as possible. Get to know each other, find ways to get along. She'll be dropping by after the shopping expedition. Maybe you could start this afternoon?"

There was an unusually long pause. "Right."

"You be nice to her, Wilbur. You're going to have to be more verbal than you are inside me."

"I imagine so."

"You might even try to be . . . charming."

"I lived longer than you have, Mike. I know a thing or two about women."

"Well, that's good to know. I thought you had perhaps forgotten. Maybe she could take you for a horse-

*back ride later on, find a nice shady spot to hang out?
She likes children's games. Catholicism too. She attended the church in Las Sombras. She has an unusual
sense of humor. For example, she —"*

"That's quite enough advice, Mike."

"I want you two to have a good time."

"Michael!"

It was a good time to break off our little talk. If
you haven't noticed, I'm not much on idleness.
I'm not the kind of person who wants to go somewhere nice and "do nothing all day long." Don't
let the grass grow under your feet, my father used
to say, for soon enough it will be growing over
your head. So I looked for a job. I had just finished sweeping the patio when I heard a car out
front and soon two female voices. The women
were back.

I helped bring the numerous bags and boxes into the house. When the essentials had been
stowed away, I offered Shy and Valentina cold
beers. We returned to the back porch. Cheyenne
had already told her mother about some of our
dealings with the Crowley ghost. Together we
filled in gaps until Valentina knew the whole
story. I gave her a sketchy version of my idea, far
from settled at this point, about how she and Wilbur could in tandem thwart Crowley's ambitions.

Val assured us that she was eager to help. "I feel useless most of the time," she confessed, "as if my time had run out and I were already dead. I've felt dead for most of my life. But when my Silver Angel was with me, death had a voice. Death had plans and the will to carry them out. Now death seems a big junkyard where the throwaways pile up."

I let her know that the happiness of our entire team depended on this job. I warned her of the risks. Should the plan fail, she could very well lose her life. But Valentina was adamant: she wanted more than anything to be useful to the living, and possible consequences were insignificant next to that.

"We're under time constraints as well. We have to be back in Ventura by next Wednesday. You two need to break the ice, learn to get along with each other. Do you think I could park Wilbur with you for the night? I'll come over tomorrow morning to pick him up."

Valentina seemed a little flustered. "My, it's been such a long time! Maybe I should freshen up? At least get my thoughts in order? You're always so logical, so intellectual, Mike. I hope he won't find me boring and scatterbrained."

"I'll vouch for Wilbur, Valentina. He's not prone to idle chatter, but outside of that you'll find him a polite and accommodating ghost."

Shy touched her mother's shoulder. "It'll be fine. Just be yourself, mother."

Valentina shot her daughter a withering glance. "Do you take me for a fool? Not much point in being anything else when a ghost comes into your mind."

"Wilbur?"

"Yes."

"Time to pass over. Let me announce your coming first."

"If you're ready, Val, so is he."

Valentina got to her feet. She was wearing a full skirt of white muslin and a light blue cotton blouse. "Please do come in, Wilbur. You're entirely welcome."

I didn't feel anything. Valentina turned away, and walked several steps. She looked back, grinning. "He's in." Then strolled off into the yard chuckling, apparently to herself.

"My," I said under my breath, "*that* was a success."

"What matchmakers we are," Cheyenne replied, landing a sisterly kiss on my cheek. Then she eyed me more coldly. "This had better be a good plan, Mike."

The next morning I decided to visit Billy Steele before driving out to the house to check in on Wilbur and Valentina. I wanted to borrow some books from his occult library and kick a few ideas around.

I found him in the Ghost Killers Clubhouse, an immense room at the back of a prefab warehouse on the Steele family ranch, which abutted the Griswold Ranch in Black Ash Canyon. Before his recent business success and bestselling book, Billy had supported himself by repairing large pieces of farm equipment in the front two-thirds of the warehouse. Today, that business was defunct. Metal shelves holding his growing library on paranormal subjects had been allowed to spread from the clubhouse into the former garage.

"Do you mind if look in the garage—maybe I should call it the library—for a book or two? My own library is in boxes beneath sheets of canvas. Then, if it's convenient, perhaps we can have a talk?"

"I'll be waiting."

"Be right with you, then."

I was delighted to find John Symonds's famously negative biography of Crowley, *The Great Beast*, published soon after the magus's death. For decades this book served as the main introduction to

Crowley for English-speakers. Its disapproving tone seemed not to have mattered in the end. Crowley's transgressive life still managed to strike a chord in some readers. They went from Symonds to Crowley's own works, and a few of them wound up dedicating their lives to Crowleyan projects.

From the same rack I selected Colin Wilson's *The Nature of the Beast*. Given my experience with other of Wilson's biographies, I expected this one to be an intelligent, thorough, but predictable critique by an author sympathetic to the occult. Also, Wilson had a good eye for the telling biographical detail passed over in silence by unobservant predecessors.

I then browsed the relatively small section on witchcraft and black magic. I chose *The Satanic Bible* by Anton Szandor LaVey, the San Francisco occultist who founded the Church of Satan and parades around in a Halloween devil costume in Kenneth Anger's *Invocation of My Demon Brother*. Nearby I noticed a copy of Blanche Barton's *The Secret Life of a Satanist*, the 'authorized' biography of LaVey. I took that one too. I hoped to learn an interesting fact or two about the consequences of pursuing a career as a black magician.

I looked for, but did not find, material on Roger Bacon, the medieval precursor of these modern magi.

Billy Steele was a pragmatic man. He prepared carefully for our ghost hunts. He was aces in situations involving fear and danger. There was a signature heroic cast to his self-presentation. A Billy Steele jacket was an unwinding cultural allusion. He wore traditions. The most recent example of his style was the Creep Jeep. Here was a vehicle widely disdained today for its fuel-guzzling, militarist personality. The companies that built it had confessed their shame, and were doing penance in the form of tin-can hybrids and electrics. The last politician to enjoy his Hummer was probably Arnold Schwarzenegger. But when Billy drove up in that Sedona red late model Hummer, the unwieldy crate was reborn as a throne car for retro masculinity. Billy saw opportunities for self-expression where others saw only embarrassment. I envied his eye.

For all the energy that Steele poured into preparation and style, there was plenty left over for the intellectual side of ghost hunting. He read modern paranormal literature, but was by no means a great respecter of it. I was grateful for this side of his personality, especially when I needed to have my ideas knocked into shape. I've never had a thought that was not improved by Billy Steele's reactions to it.

"I'm not sure we can master Crowley," I began. "Have you ever faced a more powerful ghost? Every time I think back on that demon from the abyss I feel nauseous again."

"It was impressive, all right. It was *meant* to be impressive."

"Yeah?"

"He's obviously a bad dude, Mike. But what we saw in the conjuring room might have been a piece of ghostly stage magic. We know that ghosts can design and fashion an eidolon of themselves, the 'apparition' that we 'see.' We know they can design other fearful visions. That quicksilver mine in Black Ash Canyon had several terrifying hallucinations waiting for us. Where is the Tenth Aethyr, for crying out loud? What if Crowley, in the guise of calling in Choronzon from out there in left field, simply activated a vision prepared in advance?"

"You really think that he designed that ghastly stream of facial expressions? Didn't you smell the stench?"

He shook off my worries with a shrug. "Ghosts are good at special effects. All ghosts want to appear more powerful than they are. They use their visionary powers to make us weak with fear. Lots of ghost reports mention a signature odor when the spirit appears."

"If Choronzon was a special effect, he had been seamlessly inserted into reality."

"*Seamlessly*? Maybe not quite. You told me afterwards that Crowley's reflection in the mirror seemed to blink and jump like a bad print. From where I was sitting, I could see Choronzon in the mirror. The reflection wasn't continuous. It flickered, just as you described the Crowley reflection. Maybe both Crowley and Choronzon were, so to speak, made of the same stuff."

"The stuff that dreams are made on."

"Yeah, *that* stuff. A test might have settled the matter. Had one of us touched Choronzon, that would have told us something. The thing was so odious looking that none of us tried—except for Solly. He stood up, got that chair cocked behind his back, and was ready to deliver a blow. He would either have smacked the demon or . . . knifed right through his baseless image and smacked the floor. But Crowley, you'll recall, stopped the test. I don't think he used magic to do it, either. Just the force of his authority concentrated in the word 'Stop!' I'm not saying Crowley is a complete phony or a pushover. He put a spell on our imaginations. I'm still in the grip of those dreams. But, even assuming there *are* demons in undiscovered abysses of the universe, he might *not* be able to conjure them."

I was impressed, but strong aversion prevented me from conceding his point. "Maybe you kept a clearer head than I did. Speaking of which, that headache I got on the way out wasn't an apparition."

"No. Might have been a drug, though. Perhaps smeared on the projector?"

I gave up. "I doubt that. But you could be right about Choronzon. Actually, this borders on the subject I was trying to raise at the start of this conversation. How powerful is Crowley? Does he know how to possess a human consciousness, like the Black Ash Canyon ghost?

"He said that he had a way of taking sexual well-being out of our minds. But he could do that with a spell, couldn't he? Without actually entering our minds? I talked to Wilbur yesterday. He says that the secret of possessing a human being is generally passed from one ghost to another. Before Sarka inherited this house, the Crowley spirit probably spent most of his time in a film can in a storage locker. Since then he's been cooped up in Sarka's tower. I'm thinking that Crowley may not yet have encountered a ghost, and consequently could not possibly know that secret."

Billy nodded. "Ghosts aren't gregarious. Generally speaking, they don't make alliances with other ghosts. Ghosts may return as a couple or in a small group. They might have died together. They might share a desire for revenge, or a desire to expose a hidden secret. Mostly, though, they're loners. Even if there are other ghosts in Folly's Cove, they probably steer clear of Crowley."

I remembered the vision I had seen the night Billy left me alone on the guest cottage's deck—a naked woman slipping quietly into the waters out on the edge of Folly's Cove.

"I agree, and I'm hoping we can make use of that fact. His motives appear to be entirely self-centered. No evidence of collaboration there. Crowley is one of those spirits that Drivell speculated about in that passage of his where, as you pointed out, Billy, he for a moment makes sense. The magician lusts for fame. You could construe it as a form of revenge. The world didn't give him enough of its regard when he was alive. Disappointment became wrath, and he's come back determined as all hell to get his fair share, which is more fame than anyone has ever had, Jesus Christ in particular."

Billy nodded his confirmation. "Yeah, this fellow wants to exorcize Christianity from the world and install Satan and himself in its place. Any chance we could get at least a handful of earth from Crowley's grave? It's tangible proof that the body rested, and induces in some ghosts the strong desire to lay down and give peace a chance. At the risk of psychobabble, I figure that behind every ghost is a traumatic refusal to die. Not for me, Grim Reaper! Too much to set straight! Strike hard enough at that refusal, and you can defeat any spook."

"No chance of grave dirt in this case. There was no grave. Crowley had himself cremated. The urn wound up in the hands of a supporter on the East Coast. He claimed to have dispersed the ashes somewhere in his New Jersey farm. But who knows? I'm afraid that's a dead end."

I took Billy through my plans, which were getting clearer by the minute. He heard me out in silence.

"That's some plan," Billy said. "I thought at first you were relying on Valentina, but by the end I realized that Wilbur will be the deciding factor. Frankly, I'm not sure how I feel about that. How well do you actually know your grandfather?"

"Quite well, in a sense. He thinks of my life and my strengths as a plausible unfolding of his life and his strengths. He approves of me, and since he knows me from the inside, his approval is one of my goals and rewards. I'd trust him with my life. In another sense, not well at all. Though he is in a position to do so, he doesn't ever *possess me* in the conventional way. He's more like God, in that he leaves me free and alone. I'm not sure what he does with his time. Zip around outside me, learning about things? Or hibernate within me, forever restructuring what he already knows? I don't ask him. If he wanted me to know, he would already have told me."

"Well, you're giving this diffident spirit quite a lot of responsibility. The end of your plan bothers me. Crowley might revert completely to his unholy ambitions. There's no element of compulsion."

"That's true. I couldn't figure out how we could actually compel him to behave. If we *convince* him, then fine. If not, I guess we challenge him on the matter of punishing us and hope cool reason prevails. We have this much on our side: during his life Crowley never killed, raped, or forced compliance from anyone."

"Maybe we can do more." Billy explained his revision. What he had in mind could very well fail, since it depended on the actions of another entity, but I didn't see how it could hurt us. I agreed immediately to his suggestion. The plan looked better now, with more power packed into its moment of truth. We worked on the details for a while.

Ben Griswold greeted me at the ranch. Val and Wilbur had gone riding. "I don't know what's going on in there, but it feels like a couple of ten-year-olds who have been given a new puppy and sent off on their first date. I think they were up all night. You never hear anything from the ghost, but Val was breaking out with the giggles or reciting the rhyming parts of old games. If I were younger I might feel jealous. But there's no point in envying a puff of air."

He offered coffee.

"I can't bring out her little girl mischief anymore," he confessed as we were settling down.

"Do you play games with her?"

He rose and opened a cabinet. It was packed with board games. I saw Monopoly, Jeopardy, Clue, Taboo, Trivial Pursuit, Loaded Questions, Stratego, Say Anything, Dominion, The Dating Game, The Newlywed Game, Smart Ass, and an antique version of The Game of Life.

"We play games every night. I kid her about her Scrabble words all the time. She's always trying to pawn off some ancient piece of slang, like *baldie* meaning a haircut or *fibboner* meaning someone who wants to get ahead. The other night she insisted, contra every dictionary in the house, that *bonzo* meant killing yourself in a fire. But when I rib her about this kind of thing, she doesn't get flirty and naughty. She gets mad and frustrated."

"Well," I said, knowing my remark would be pointless, "she's been through a lot of trauma in the last year."

"So have I. But hell, maybe the puff of air will do her some good. Maybe going to Ventura and trying to teach your new ghost a lesson will do her some good. Myself, I'm at a loss, Mike. Nothing works, and I don't know what to do."

When Val returned from her ride, Ben excused himself and went to the barn to work in his shop.

I walked outside. Val already had the saddle off her white-maned palomino.

"Were you with Ben just now?"

"Yeah. He went over to the barn to work on saddles."

"I'll be over there in a minute myself. Listen Mike, I've had a wonderful time with Wilbur! He curls up so quietly sometimes that I don't even know for sure whether he's there. But not like a cat. It's a *strong presence*, Mike, really a *strong presence*."

"I've got a clearer idea now of what you two are preparing for. I brought over some training exercises that you could run through."

"Training exercises! What fun!"

"I hope you continue to feel that way. I'm going to reclaim Wilbur for a moment or two. He'll tell you all about the modified plan."

I put my back to Valentina.

"God, Mike. Women. It's sooo nice to get a break. But she does have big reserve tanks of grit and determination. Watch yourself, Aleister Crowley! She's also learned some tricks from her years with the Herrera ghost. Crowley has her in education, book learning, world travel, cultural literacy, and a thousand other categories. But she knows ghosts damn well."

"And you? You're immune to her charms?"

"No. I wouldn't say that."

"Her husband wouldn't either. He called you 'a puff of air,' but made it clear that he was jealous of you nonetheless."

"A live human should never envy a ghost. He has a body."

"Jealousy never stops at realism."

"True."

"I've changed the plan some, Wilbur." I explained in detail. *"Make sure that Val understands the new wrinkles. I also thought up a training exercise. You pretend you are Aleister Crowley. Go through a range of plausible responses to various stages of our little drama. Try each one several times. Encourage Val to be inventive, ingenious. Then discuss the long-term effects of each of her postures. Evaluate them. Throw*

out the lousy ones. Highlight the ones that move Crow-ley in favorable directions. I think you and Val may enjoy this game."

"I guess I'd better go to work."

"Bye bye."

I turned back toward Valentina. She smiled at me and tipped her hat, then began walking her horse toward the barn. After a few steps I heard her chuckle. It may well have been her response to the idea of Wilbur pretending to be Aleister Crow-ley.

I gave him two days, then went over to our guest cottage and picked him up.

"I need you back, Wilbur. I want to cram your mind with facts about Crowley's life."

"I have already absorbed many of them."

"Well, I have some new ones," I said, and thought back over my memories of the last two days' worth, just to give him a quick idea of the size of his task.

Knowledge is power shall be the whole of the law.

CHAPTER NINE

Shy and I decided that, since Valentina was accompanying us to Ventura, we would take our own car. We drove from New Aarhus to Lassiter Springs on Wednesday morning.

Ben had wanted no part of the trip or its mission. He helped an excited yet skittish Valentina prepare for the trip, and stood by in silence as we loaded her luggage. His wife clung to him in a long embrace before lowering herself into the back seat of our Mercedes SUV. As we were almost ready to depart, Billy and Solly shot up our driveway trailing an impressive plume of dust. We left a few minutes later with the Mercedes in the lead. Better the Creep Jeep eat our dust than the other way around.

We made good time for most of the trip. Wilbur rode inside Val, the two of them working in secret on their final flourishes. I didn't want to distract them, so kept my hands off the car's remarkable sound system. There was no chuckling today. I occasionally caught Val in the rearview mirror, her eyes closed, having what I imagined to be an intent thought talk with her companion. We ran into a road work bottleneck just outside of Ventura, which cost us nearly an hour, and pulled into Folly's Cove around noon.

Marta greeted us and once again handed over the keys to the guest house. I took her aside.

"How has he been?"

"Confident, but with signs of nervousness. He fears *you*."

"I saw him that night after we had talked on the patio."

She nodded. "We saw you out there. I told you what I wanted you to know. I didn't lie to you. Obviously, there was more—things I didn't want you to know. When I saw you out there in the rain spying on us, I felt violated."

"If Crowley had threatened you with cancer and other afflictions for failing to contribute to his sexual well-being, you might feel *really* violated."

"No apology for eavesdropping on us?"

I felt very clear about my answer. "No." The image of a hangdog Crowley staring helpless and forlorn at Marta's panties had been the key inspiration for today's venture.

A rumpled, unshaven Robby Sarka was there, looking like death warmed over. Billy had called him yesterday with the news that we had a plan in place. He withheld most of the details. There wasn't any point in seeking Robby's advice. Young Sarka was too obsessed with the choices

Crowley had imposed on him to be helpful on strategy.

Robby Sarka, Billy Steele, and Solly Barlow were to stay in the living room of the main house. The four remaining guests would climb the stairs to the magical chamber at the top. The Magnificent Four: me, Cheyenne, Valentina, and Wilbur, who was to appear as a separate and distinct apparition.

In writing these tales of the Ghost Killers I have never described Wilbur's materialization. I had in fact never seen it before. He appeared as a clean-shaven man of fifty wearing a three-piece light gray suit. His reddish brown hair was familiar, since its genetic offspring was growing on my own skull. His ears were smaller, his nose larger. But his blue eyes had passed on to me. Shy told me once that I had a way of putting a glint in my eyes that made men respect me and women want to mother me. When Wilbur and I looked eye to eye for a moment, I saw the glint.

In my childhood memories Wilbur was an older man. But his face still conveyed a peculiar double concentration, here in the present yet also far away, and his apparition moved with the strange economy I remembered. Wilbur always had a way of not calling attention to himself. He would be sitting in a room with you. You turned to say something and he was gone. I glimpsed a comparable stealth as he spoke inaudibly to Valentina and they began ascending the turret staircase. Cheyenne and I followed half a floor behind.

When we arrived at the magician's den, Wilbur was already introducing himself and his escort.

"I'm Wilbur Buckman, Mr. Crowley, and this is Valentina Griswold, Cheyenne Buckman's mother. Doubtless you've sensed that I'm a fellow ghost. We lot know each other at once. I beheld your last performance through my grandson's eyes, but today I wanted to meet you openly."

Crowley looked down with a quizzical *hauteur*. "'Fraid I've never seen a ghost before. I assume you're not going to make a rival offer?"

"Sharp of you—or were you being supercilious? I did hope that I could clear up some matters concerning ghosts and sex."

"Oh, dear," Val said. "You make it sound so formal and so cold!"

"Val here is the place to start. She had long-term dealings with a ghost, and might be able to open your eyes to certain possibilities."

Crowley looked her over. Valentina's soft white dress showed off her butternut coloring, and looked well with the silver hair flowing down from her sun bonnet. But given what I knew of him, the living Crowley would not have selected a woman like Valentina for his consort. She was too old, clean, naive, reserved. You never knew, though. Maybe becoming a ghost, as profoundly as being born, changes a man.

"The best thing," Val said, "would be for you to come in for a visit—that is, if you could spare the time."

Crowley looked confused. "Do you own a house near here?"

She flushed with embarrassment. "No, I mean *in*, in my mind."

Here Wilbur took over again. I knew he found the role of pander distasteful, but he was managing to exude the casual smarminess his part demanded. "It's a trick that some ghosts learn. You can enter a person's mind. Once there? Well, there are things we ghosts can't do alone. Let me show you."

"But I have deals to make." He looked from Cheyenne to Mike. Then he spoke to Mike. "Where are the rest of you?"

"Downstairs," I answered.

Wilbur stepped closer to Crowley. "Forget your meeting for a little while. The Ghost Killers aren't going anywhere. Robby is down there too. Why does Mona Lisa smile? What do women want? You can find out right now, this very afternoon."

Crowley's eyes narrowed. "And what will you be gaining from this act of charity?"

Wilbur's reply had the transferred self-righteousness of early Iago. "I just thought that a spook of your distinction would want to understand all dimensions of ghost sex before signing a deal meant to enhance his sexual energy."

It wasn't long before Wilbur, and then Crowley, disappeared.

Time for a private word, readers. After the events of this chapter transpired, I interviewed Wilbur and Valentina. I made use of both their memories in writing this narrative, though I chose to tell the tale from Wilbur's point of view. Perhaps, since he is male, my direct ancestor, and as a ghost my lifelong (albeit mostly silent) companion, the choice requires no further explanation. But I do feel that his viewpoint is for the story's sake the most advantageous.

For the remainder of this chapter, I pass the narrative baton to my father's father, Wilbur Buckman.

I popped in.

I had just shown Crowley how to do it. A ghost has to be near the target. Dematerializing, he seeks through meditation to annihilate his presence. This "self-blanking" can never of course be perfect, since the center of consciousness cannot think itself out of existence. I think therefore I am, like the man said. Then, with about one quarter of his will power, he scoots forward. And he's in.

I knew from Mike's absurdly detailed research that Crowley had spent years practicing Eastern techniques of meditation and adapting them to traditional magical practices such as astral travel. I was confident that he would be along soon.

"Hello?" a disoriented Crowley said.

He was answered by an ebullient Valentina. "Please, make yourselves at home! As you can see, I'm leaving that stuffy tower. I thought we would be more comfortable down at the beach."

Mike and Valentina had accompanied us just in case something went wrong, but thus far everything was copacetic. We left them in the third-floor chamber. Let the party begin.

We ghosts had full access to the visual and aural dimensions of Val's sensorium. She walked down the turret stairs, out the side door of the house, and down the beach stairs, stopping to select a lounge chair from a large plastic container. She chose a sandy spot. Adjusting the lounge, she lay down and savored the view. It was a cloudless afternoon. Swells rose on the outer edge of the cove, lifting ropes of kelp into the sunlight, then became small waves sculpted by an off-shore breeze. Val lowered the brim of her hat. The shade must have felt delicious.

"You have the use of my imagination, Mr. Crowley. Materialize, if you would. I long to see you."

I took the lead, opening a vague but roomy space in Val's imagination and materializing there. Val arrived, looking significantly younger than she had from outside. She wore a dark red tunic with a silver belt and strappy silver heels. Crowley appeared beside her in one of his astrological robes, this time with his famous motto "Do as thou wilt shall be the whole of the law" embroidered over the heart.

"So you are frustrated, Aleister? Terribly frustrated? Perhaps I can help. Long ago, with *my* ghost, who was my grandfather Bernardino Herrera, I found ways to settle him down. I can show you a few of them, if you like. We can't actually touch. The frustration won't go away. My technique is to concentrate on that, and see if it can't be turned in a pleasure."

"Please!" Crowley exclaimed.

"Frustration is a given for all ghosts," I added, underlining the facts of ghost life. "We don't eat, we don't sleep, we don't touch."

"Many's the thing we don't do, and it's a terrible nuisance," Crowley scoffed. "I try to complete a simple enchantment spell, using the best text from the most reliable grimoire, and there I am, incanting away, and sure enough, the magician is told to spit into the incense bowl. I continue on, but it seems that human spit is the effective agent in this spell. I find another text that does not involve spit, but this version asks instead for the magician's tears. I would say that it's a bloody pain in the ass, but not having a body *isn't that*, alas."

"Magic is for the living," I said.

Crowley glanced at me warily. "In some respects, yes."

Val frowned at me for a moment, then turned back with a smile to Crowley, as if I were a hopeless killjoy. "Best to dwell, don't you think, on what you *can* do? Bernardino said that physical existence seem closer and more intense when he was 'riding my thoughts.' Try to attach yourself to the pulse of my thinking. There's a life rhythm in here. 'Your thoughts have body,' Bernardino would say. Saddle up, Aleister. Get astride me. Give your mind to me."

Crowley's materialization had begun to tremble slightly. Val was working her magic on him, as she had on me during my first hours in her.

"Better! Now, back to your frustration. It isn't really about spit, is it? Here's the simple truth, Aleister. You can bid farewell to the flesh, learn to do without it, or you can eroticize your frustration. You used to do that quite lot when alive, or so I've heard. Delayed orgasms, that kind of thing? In those days there was always a consummation waiting for you after the frustration. Not now. You don't have a heartbeat or blood to push around. You don't have a dick. But let's pretend. . .."

She walked right up to Crowley and put her hands on the dick spot of his apparition. "I don't want you to have a normal dick like living men. It made you think nasty thoughts and do nasty things. You couldn't control it. That's why I locked you in this cock cage. It's steel, shiny high-gloss steel, and I've closed it with a special pen-tangle padlock made before World War II by Sarka Locks. The key is on a chain around my neck, resting between my breasts. The cage is only three inches long. And tight. I have them in all sizes, by the way."

"God! Satan! I can feel a bone-on!"

I looked down and they had imagined it all in-to being. Crowley's dick was cramped inside a stringent cage held in place by a beautiful little padlock in the shape of a five-pointed star. His pelvis spasmed with frustration.

Crowley's neediness was pathetic. It was as if he had died this morning. There had been no intervening self-discipline, no stoicism, no attempt, as Mike might say, to "man up" to a ghost's situation. Just the opposite. Crowley had been doing everything possible to provide himself with the bounties of a real sex life. Our plan was to make use of his raw needs. Still, it was impossible not to feel a little sorry for the spirit. Mike doesn't realize how difficult a subject the penis is for a male ghost. When something sexual is going on, I leave my grandson to himself. I prefer not to talk about it either. Too painful.

But Crowley was in good hands now. Valentina. . . . I'll just say that she had been a revelation to me as well.

"You're fighting the bone-on because there isn't enough room in the cage. But you seem to be losing the fight, for your cock is bulging out from the edges of its cage. You mustn't expect mercy, Aleister. This is permanent. Delay is forever."

Again his apparition's pelvis shook. The padlock chimed against the bars of the cage. "No! You Scarlet Whore, you Bitch of Hell! Colder than Laura, Crueler than Wanda!"

"Who's Laura and Wanda? But not so cold as all that. I bet you are abject and lusty enough that you could be made to dribble pre-cum in there, and beg me for the privilege. Should you in fact prove able to ejaculate in your cage, I have a urethral plug that can be screwed through this little round opening at the top." She held up the shiny plug. It was perhaps an inch and a half long and bent to fit the curvature that the cage imposed on Crowley's imaginary cock. Then she put her finger on his urethra. She had reimagined her hands with long scarlet nails, and worked the one on her index finger into the tip of his cock. "Then you could be eternally frustrated! In fact, let's screw the plug in your man-slit and see how well it fits."

Crowley shook some more, now in a delirium of teased-up frustration. The padlock clinked and clanked against the cage. Valentina gently but firmly inserted the plug through urethral hole at the end of the cock cage and tightened it with a few flicks of her wrist.

"A perfect fit! That should hold those dribbles back."

My cue. I stepped up to the backside of Crowley, reaching around to show him a good-sized steel butt plug. "Your favorite configuration in life, I believe? Two men and a woman? I don't think your frustration could possibly be complete until we have filled this other hole. Next to your mouth, it is the least well behaved of your orifices, is it not? You have a bad bad dick, but a worse asshole."

Val laughed at him. "You need *double dip* chastity!"

"Yes, yes, you sweet tarts," Crowley whispered, tears streaming down his materialization's face. "Do anything to me. I'm worthless shit. . . . Sometimes I hate myself."

I stepped around in front of Crowley and put my arm on Val's shoulder. "He called himself 'The Beast,' Val. You've put him in a cage, which is where any beast belongs. Shall we finish the job? Perhaps he might like to watch us copulate."

I knew that Crowley had enjoyed being humiliated by both women and men, especially men, but to see how enthusiastically he responded to our impositions was shocking. After we had fitted him in a filling butt plug, we displayed him for each other's pleasure and peppered our routines with taunts, slights, and demands. When asked to show more enthusiasm, he whinnied like a stallion or yelped like a puppy. We seemed to have tapped into the proverbial bottomless well. I recalled that Crowley had promised to those who signed Faustian agreements "a complete map" of his sexual desires. It was clear that no such map currently existed. The man could spend eternity tracing the ways and byways of his self-abasement alone.

Val and I were ready for rational discussion. We unimagined the sexual devices. Crowley brought them right back into existence. We unimagined them again, and again Crowley remade them. I thought of Blake's famous line about "mind-forg'd manacles."

Val shook her head in exasperation. "You're being awfully trying!" She turned to me. "Have you ever seen a ghost this shameless, Wilbur?" She was in fine form, so I let her flow on. She removed the urethral plug from his cock. "There's one last thing you can do for me. I know that image-of-a-dick down there won't be able to feel any of this, but I want you to show me one drop of precum and one drop only."

"I want to spurt!"

"One drop, I said!"

Moaning and begging, thrusting and shaking and shuddering, Mr. Crowley finally emitted a single futile drib of precum. It welled out like a tear.

"Good boy, Aleister. But that's quite enough for now."

I seconded the sentiment. "Hot diggity dog ziggity, Al. You've been taken to the cleaners. No more sex for you today."

The sex paraphernalia disappeared. Crowley composed himself.

"Pay attention, my good sir," Val began, her expression close to intolerant exasperation. "I have shown you a possibility open to ordinary ghosts. Some find a human host. Wilbur, for example, lives in his grandson Mike Buckman. When circumstances require it, they converse, and Wilbur shares what he wishes to share with his grandson. Otherwise, they lead a quiet life. Wilbur wants Mike free to be himself at every moment.

"If you find a host or part-time host with an interest in ghost sex, you can live a more passionate existence, such as Bernardino enjoyed with me."

Crowley hesitated a moment, then said it anyway. "You two also had the *frisson*, and the old tragic depth, of incest. A story fit for the Greek stage, I'm sure!"

For Crowley, incest was the most ennobling feature of Valentina's relationship with her grandfather. But he *did* have a point, I suppose. You had to have done something impressively taboo to gain the attention of a Greek tragedian.

"I hope to acquire energies that will allow me to continue my poetry," Crowley persisted. "I could immortalize you! You speak as though I would have to *find* a sexual host. I have found my host. I am inside her now."

Val shook her head. "Out of the question. I'm a seventy-year-old married woman with a vigorous husband and a sympathetic family ghost whom I expect to host now and then in the years remaining to me."

She did? This remark had not surfaced in our rehearsals. I thought she was going to tell Crowley that she just wasn't attracted to him. She *had* done that, but in casting me as a preferable rival dipped Crowley's rejection in a poison of humiliating jealousy.

Those remaining years sounded interesting.

"It cannot be. To find you and lose you on the same afternoon? Devastating! Unbearable!"

"There you have it," Valentina said.

It was my job to point Crowley toward reduced horizons. "You're acting like a spoiled child, Aleister. What of Marta? Not as experienced as Val, but game I would think. She'll learn the ropes."

"A mere housekeeper!"

During his lifetime Crowley had never outgrown a childish self-absorption. He had been far more interested in himself than in the world. It had hindered him fatally as a poet and novelist. Now the same vainglory was ruining his spirit life.

"You mustn't sneer at her, Aleister. She associates you with Benedek, and considers it to be her duty to show you hospitality. And she has, I think you know, a large heart for hospitality. Without her you don't have a chance in hell of enjoying companionship. Do you have family?"

Crowley winced. "Perhaps a few relatives of former wives are still groping about somewhere. I did want an heir! I never thought much of Ataturk, though my reunion with the boy at the end of my life gave me a temporary lift. But that door is closed." Crowley paced back and forth, sulking. He turned suddenly toward me, fire in his eyes. "*You* have a strong young host. What happens when your grandson dies? Do you find another, then another?"

"No. That's not for me. Mike knew me and loved me during his childhood. I can be of use to him and to those he cares for. When he dies, no one alive will remember the living me. At that point I'll give up the ghost."

I stopped to let the last sentence sink in. It was our first mention of ghosts dying. Crowley got it, all right, but not fully. He gazed at me in utter contempt.

"Were the motives that made you a ghost in the first place so paltry as that? Why *did* you become a ghost?"

"I haven't told that story in years. Mike's never heard it. I certainly don't intend to tell it to you. But yes, those motives now seem paltry and out-moded to me. They arose from circumstances that no longer hold. Water under the bridge. The world moves on. Someday, somehow, the piper must be paid. Most of us spirits don't last for more than a generation."

For a moment Crowley seem stunned. He hadn't realized that. The bad news struck him like a stiff shot of liquor, and he blinked it down. But again his response was defiant. "Going gently into that goodnight, are you? Rot, then! I'll have none of your cringing self-effacement. I'm made of the sternest stuff of all: will of the devil. I'll do every-thing I couldn't do in life. If I need extra will, I'll get it."

"You're referring to your harebrained scheme of using a team of human Fausts as a sexual bat-tery?"

"Yes! And rather more noble than your bour-geois aspiration to mope inside some relative for a generation, then die again."

"You've had an energy-sharing pact with Benedek Sarka?"

"Why do you need to ask? You were present, hiding inside Michael Buckman, during my demonstration last week. You know I had a contract with Benedek."

"And what has it enabled you to accomplish?"

"Much! Very much! At first I was attached to the film of my death. When the movie was being projected, I could travel from the film to the screen. Gradually I willed myself to separate from the movie and inhabit the entire third-floor. As I fed on Sarka's energies, my dominion spread, first to the two lower rooms, then to the house as a whole. Now I move about the grounds."

"Tell me, Aleister. It must be a month or perhaps two or three months since you fed on fresh energies from Sarka. He was winding down to death. He can't have been filled with libidinal well-being; his sex pep must have been declining for years. Did you notice any weakening during this time?"

"Not at all. It's a measure of my strength. I've pulled myself up by my bootstraps, and I still have a long way to go."

There he was, proud of his strength and expecting more. Mike had coached me over and over on the handling of this precise moment. Now was the time to deliver my bombshell.

"I hate to burst your bubble, Aleister, but these transfusions of libidinal well-being? These heroin fixes from the living? They have never given you *a goddamn thing*. Nada. That's why your power has not weakened in the last years or months. You never did get power from Sarka. You won't get any stronger if you enslave a whole metropolis of Fausts."

His jerked back, huffing and puffing. The eyes bored into me. His head shot toward mine like a striking snake. I had questioned his most precious assumption, and he loathed me for it.

"You insult me to the quick, sir! You will need to be corrected! How could a dirt-ignorant milk-sop possibly know such a thing?"

He pulled away. My apparition pushed right back into his face. "Because I know ghosts, and you don't!"

It took a few moments for both of us to calm down. "Look," I resumed, "you became a spirit through the filming of your death. The most poignant moment in that movie is when you croak, and the women who was tending you hears a gust of wind smack the window and says 'The gods are greeting him.' They might have greeted you—other spirits from your culture might have greeted you—had you not died on film. Your will was committed to the film experiment, the pentangle lens, the Hollywood world where your magical lodge in Pasadena had the best opportunity of surviving your death. So you awoke in an artificial tower by the California coast with no native ghosts to show you the way. All you had was your own hyperbolic fantasies, and you gave them free rein.

"The fact is that every ghost begins with a deep connection to a particular place or surrounding, and only gradually learns to roam free of it. Valentina's ghost, for example. Herrera was an incredibly strong spirit. He controlled, besides Valentina, another young man and a second ghost. For all his power, it took him over ninety years to migrate a few hundred yards. It has taken you—what? Sixty-nine years to make it from the film in the tower to the front lawn and the beach! Your increased reach since death is just the usual expected enlargement of a ghost's haunts. It would have happened without any transfusions. It *did* happen without the transfusions. They made no difference whatsoever."

Crowley was obviously shaken. My bombshell had landed right on his core confusion. "But . . . my plans! I am risen, the world shall revere me!"

I laughed. "Yes, your ridiculous plans. Alive, you thought yourself a great poet, a major religious prophet, a man of power. The world never showed the slightest inclination to agree with you. Now that you're a ghost, your unsatisfied appetite for recognition—call it fame-lust—is going to suffer the same frustration as your physical lust.

"Don't you suppose that other ghosts have aspired to world-wide popularity? Have had the fantasy of becoming the spiritual leader of the world with an endearing populist touch or two? Open your eyes, Crowley. You're not the first fame-crazed son of Eve to come back a ghost. They all found out what you will find out. To wit, no ghost could keep up a schedule like you imagine. Just try staying materialized for a full day! I see you know what I mean. Takes it out of you, doesn't it, and leaves you weak for days afterward? If he wants to make a splash, the best a spirit can do is haunt one place with some regularity and now and then pull off a frightening materialization. Moreover, we're talking here about ghosts that are genuinely vengeful. That means focused. You're pissed off, but at too broad a target. The world, the universe? Successful ghosts have it in for that man, that woman. In your case, you didn't get everything you wanted from life. Boo fucking hoo. It's nothing but the common human lot. You're just another ghost whose outsized revenge project cannot and will not get off the ground.

214

"We don't have that much power, Aleister. We can bluster, we can frighten people. If we are very nasty, we can manage an atrocity or two. But you don't want atrocities. You want fame and adulation. Ghosts cannot sustain such a frantic pace. Even if you had the battery, you couldn't take the charge."

Bludgeoning Crowley's revolve with truth upon truth seemed to be having the desired effect. He began pacing again. But now and then he would go through his robe, patting its pockets. Irritation compounded, he resumed his pacing. Of course! I had seen several photographs of the man taken in middle age. He was always smoking a large Sherlockian calabash. Ghosts don't have lungs. They can't smoke. Crowley was inventorying his frustrations. Suddenly now, at every turn, he ran up against the hard facts of his existence.

Crowley stopped walking. He seemed to concentrate on something. After a time he shook his head, frustrated again.

"Wilbur," he finally said to me in an exasperated tone. "How do I get out of here, anyway?"

"I assume you've heard of the fundamental rule, as Goethe called it? A ghost must leave a room or enclosure the same way it entered."

"I just tried that!"

"You tried to annihilate yourself? Then you punched will's gas pedal about a quarter of the way down. . . . And it didn't work?"

"No!"

"Be scientific, sir. That's how you get in, not how you get out. There's a reversal involved. Going from the outside of a window to the inside is not the same as going from the inside to the outside. Besides, you're in no mood to go any-where. You're liable to frighten someone if you go barreling around in this frame of mind. Just re-lax."

"You're holding *me* prisoner? You'll pay for this!"

"What are going to do about it? Conjure Cho-ronzon? He might not be of much use. Maybe one of his more competent cohorts?"

Crowley cut to the chase. It must have seemed superior to enduring more helplessness. "What do you want from me?"

At last. I softened my voice. "A change of atti-tude. No more grandiosity. No more threatening. No more assuming that the rules governing all other ghosts don't apply to you."

I left him to his pacing. What Mike's genera-tion would call his body language, or more pre-cisely his materialization language, told the story. Pacing back and forth always spells confinement.

I suppose he might have tried to wreak havoc on our host mind. But I felt a powerful conviction that he would not. Crowley, the great trespasser, scourge of the bourgeoisie, had inbred scruples. He wasn't about to go berserk. He paced while fantasizing going berserk. The man went in for *mental* chastity too.

I merged with Valentina's thoughts.

"We did well."

"But I feel bad that he wanted to be my consort. I could console him."

"His life was marked by short but passionate attachments. The ghost is no different. Leave him be for a while. I called his bluff on Choronzon. It appears that Billy Steele was correct, and the demon was the equivalent of a stage illusion. Magic without the k, as Crowley terms it."

"I *could* console him."

"Of course you could, my dear. But don't. Leave him be for a while. His Satanic Majesty's court magician has new truths to get through his head. You can't do that for him."

I waited till late afternoon, when Val was about to change locations, before telling Crowley how to exit a person. I wanted the location change to be a surprise, and thought that my technical lesson would provide the necessary distraction.

"See the view your host is seeing. Concentrate, not on yourself, as you did when getting in, but on some element of the visual field. That, too, if you work hard at it, is annihilating. When you know the reality of what you see, depress the gas pedal of will just enough. Maybe ten percent. Voila, out you go! You'll probably flub it up a few times. But keep trying and you'll get it. I'll go first."

Just as we had planned, Valentina was gazing at the entrance to the cave. I heard sea water being busted into foam on the rocks at her back. There appeared to be perhaps an hour of light remaining. Inside the cave mouth I could make out a portion of the energy diagram that Mike had recognized as a yantra. I concentrated on that. A little more than a little will. . . .

Presto, and out I popped. I turned around toward Val. She was at the center of our entire group. Mike and Cheyenne stood beside her, Billy and Solly beside them, with Robby Sarka on the end next to Billy.

Behind them all, hovering five yards over the sea, was the mystical queen mother. Glimmers of sunset seemed to die behind her. She was like a dark rainbow promising eternal wrath. Our compulsion had arrived.

We knew of course that powerful energies would intersect on this day. Robby Sarka and his past. Aleister Crowley and his past. Valentina Griswold and her past. We hoped this woman would appear today. Billy suggested that she would. Mike, who believed he had seen her a week ago, thought she would. I hoped he was right. There she was, by God, the answer to our prayers—and amazing!

Water streamed off the woman from no apparent source, off her dark locks, off her heavy breasts, and bounced on the ocean below. The column of water seemed almost to be holding her aloft, like a crystal pedestal. Mike had looked over a few old photographs of her. I scarcely recalled them. But I recognized her at once from her son's brown eyes and almond complexion. She nodded to me, one ghost to another. It was a really magnificent materialization.

When Crowley popped out, facing away from the water, I walked him directly into the cave. He hadn't an inkling of the otherworldly force poised above the ocean. We stopped to survey the paintings.

"I suppose she received one of your Sendings, as we call those packages of sex ideas. She stayed closer to your fantasy blueprints than any of the Ghost Killers did. Personally I never liked those arranged tableaus from the old Tantric sources, though when I sold antiques in San Francisco I had customers who coveted them. Mike vetoed that strain in your Sending. So did Shy, Billy, and Solly. But this woman was a good student, no? She painted neo-Tantric sex groupings. She sought out extra-marital partners. She had brief but passionate attachments, as with the passing yachtsman. Was the Sending addressed to her alone? Or did she just happen to receive your latest ideas for Benedek Sarka?"

Crowley seemed uncomfortable. "It was meant for Benedek. I've always regretted her death. I was bumbling around, seeking my path, without a body. My magic wasn't as precise as it should have been."

"But as you say, what does it matter? The complexities never matter." I turned toward the cave's entrance and walked out, Crowley at my side. Robby and the Ghost Killers had turned toward the sea. Crowley saw them, and her, for the first time.

"You may not recognize the naked woman manifested here, Aleister, because at the time you cast the spell that led to her cave painting and then to her death, you had limited mobility. Did you ever see her when she was alive? Perhaps you've seen her spirit from the window of your upper chamber?

"This is Allegra Malatesti Sarka, Benedek's wife and Robby's mother. She's one of those focused ghosts. Knows exactly why she's here. Allegra has come back from death to take revenge on you for what you have done to her, her husband, and her son!"

Allegra rose like a kite, till I could barely make her out against the blackening sky. Then down the same line she came with the speed of pent fury. The group scattered, racing around the corner to the safety of the cove. Don't know how she did it; never seen its like. She zipped into the water and disappeared without a splash. Then, obscuring all else, a twelve-foot pile driver of a wave sped toward the cave mouth. I knew that wall of maddened salt water would flow right through me, but instinctively I shut off my materialization. Crowley, less experienced, clambered backward, seeking shelter in the cave.

It sliced right through me. It thundered into the cave, and the white-water rebound sliced through me again, leaving a chill at the heart of my bodiless being. I got the message. It was both a command and an oath, written in furious waters, and meant for Crowley, though in the aftermath he was nowhere to be seen. DO NOT EVER LEAVE THIS PLACE.

I didn't see Crowley again until later that night, just as we were about to go. He was up in his third-floor retreat. I think he must have been pacing. He paused at the window, and that's where I beheld him for an instant.

Earlier Mike told the Ghost Killers about towers topped with book-lined studies, Montaigne's tower, Milton's tower. There was another ancient association with towers: towers are prisons. That's what I thought about when I glimpsed Crowley's restless shade looking out to sea. He'd gotten the message.

CHAPTER TEN

Mike Buckman is back on the case, readers.

Everyone was coming over to warm our newly renovated home. Val and Ben arrived first. It was only a short walk for them, of course, and they had come early to help us get ready. Fresh from the shower, dressed in one of my short-sleeved island shirts, I let them in at the kitchen door.

Val was carrying a large cake plate. She kissed me on the cheek, then pushed on by me into the kitchen, where Cheyenne would point her toward the destination appropriate for our dessert. Ben had on a fancy cowboy outfit, his white hair neatly brushed, and greeted me with a firm handshake.

I asked about drinks. Val passed for now. Ben wanted a weak g. & t. I made two of those, handing the first to him.

"You're looking good, Ben."

He tried his drink. Then he said, in a lowered voice, "I swear, Mike, ghost hunting is a miracle tonic. Ever since she got back from Ventura, she's been a different woman. Damn, but it's fun."

I surreptitiously glanced down at his fly. I wondered if there was a shiny steel cage behind that zipper? There did seem to be an unnatural bulge. . . . Maybe I was seeing things.

Val walked up with a martini in her hand. "When I saw that shaker in the fridge, I changed my mind. Nothing friendlier than a sweating martini shaker!"

She used to communicate with Wilbur through me. Now, a woman of the world in all ghost-related matters, she spoke to him directly, well aware that he was listening. "Pop in for a minute, Wilbur. I want to chat."

She slipped into the family room. Wilbur must have said something funny, because she was cack-ling away in there. Those two had a regular ar-rangement now. Wilbur spent the night in her every two weeks. Ben had gotten past his jealous phase. I had a talk with him, and made it clear that, when it came to actual sex, ghost guys not only had no bullets, but no guns either. Whatever sexual feelings Wilbur might inspire in his wife, they were his to harvest.

Billy and Solly arrived next. The drinkers moved over to the family room, where Cheyenne, busy in the kitchen, could still take part in our conversa-tion, due to the missing wall we had knocked out.

"Has anybody heard from Robby?" Shy asked.

"I called to thank him for my million dollar check," Val said. "That was so very nice of him! I never expected such a thing." When our checks arrived from Robby there had been five of them, not four. Presented with hers, Valentina lit up like Rockefeller Center at Christmas time. I told Shy later that I had seen astonishing ecstasy on her face, but had never witnessed a happier female Griswold expression than the one on her mother when she beheld that check. Her first use of the money was to order renovations to our guest cottage, which would begin next month. Shy had caught wind that Wilbur might be given his own room. Valentina was making lists of his favorite books, movies, painters. The possibility of doing that had never occurred to me.

"I talked to Robby last week," Billy said, taking a healthy draw of his Nevada Pale Ale. "He's getting married to a woman named Brandy. Man, he's happy not to be sharing her in any way with Aleister Crowley."

"We freed him of his father," I noted.

"Right," Billy came back, "who was fused with Crowley. Some father! By the way, you guys should check out Robby's website, the Fantasy Fantasy one. His programmers did indeed develop a ghost hunter figure. It comes in two genders, Stephen Weird and Susan Weird. I took them up on a free trial offer, and played along for a month as Stephen Weird. Tell you the truth, it was kind of strange. I asked Robby on the phone to fill me in on the design of the character. He finally confessed that Steve Weird was made to look like me and think like Mike. I had already known that subliminally, but now I had confirmation. I really ought to sue. As you all know, Mike is much better looking than me, and I can think rings around the guy."

Everyone found this hugely funny.

"Maybe they did basic research in maternity wards," Shy said. "I bet you all the women hoping for boys would go for the 'looks like Billy, thinks like Mike' concept."

That got another monster laugh.

"It's already been tried," Solly said. "They called him John Wayne."

Funnier and funnier.

"As my grandfather used to say," I remarked, "'damn tootin'."

Wilbur popped out, said "I *never* said 'damn tootin'!" and disappeared. That topped everything.

When the hilarity had died down, Valentina asked whether Robby intended to live at Folly's Cove.

Billy shook his head. "No way. But he's afraid to sell the place, lest Crowley work his wicked magic on the next owner. So Folly's Cove remains in the family, but is never to be inhabited again, at least in the foreseeable future."

"More of a folly than ever," Solly remarked.

Valentina wanted to know whether Marta would stay on.

Solly nodded knowingly. "I saw her last week. She's a fine companionable woman, and she says she is entirely capable of taking care of Crowley."

"I'm sure she'll do an excellent job," Shy piped up from kitchen.

"I'll send her some tips," Val said.

"Mother!"

"What I want to know is," Solly continued, "with all our talk about ghosts having no bodies and no dicks, why do I feel jealous of one?"

"Happens," Ben said.

It was a warming party, lots of laughs and lots of fellowship. But I was not unhappy to see everyone out the door, make nightcaps for Shy and me, and enjoy the comfort of our new living room.

"This case turned out to be good for everyone, Shy. Us too."

"You mean our recent sexual closeness?"

"Yeah!"

"And yeah! Those dreams may have started as Crowley's, but they ended as ours."

We drank for a bit.

"It isn't just the sex. It isn't just the greater trust we have in each other because our love survived a danger. Somehow, I don't like the idea that I was already perfect for you and you found me that way and want to preserve me that way. Or vice versa. I'm not talking about complete renovation—nothing so extreme as what we have done to the house. But I prefer . . . that I am making bits of you, and you are making bits of me, and therefore we're perfect for each other."

She thought a moment. "I think I can understand how you have shaped me. I'm reactive. But how have I shaped you?"

"Take your mother."

"You've been lovely to her, to both of them, giving them a place in our home."

"But I thought in terms of taking care of them during their sunset years. It never crossed my mind, until this case, that Valentina was central to the basic resources of the Ghost Killers. I'm not unmindful that you saw this at once."

"I didn't know she was a spirit dominatrix!"

"Maybe not. But you knew intuitively that she would understand a spirit like Crowley and be able to stand up to him and manage him."

"True. I guess it amounts to the same thing."

"The strangest thing about your mother is that she doesn't hate everything about Bernardino Herrera. She should be angrier at ghosts. I mean, you would think that like the usual trauma victim she would loathe the things she did for Herrera.

But she doesn't. They're a part of her. She enjoys her skills."

"She really does. Did it strike you that Robby's mother was in effect the avenger that my mother couldn't give us?"

"Never crossed my mind. But now that you mention it, yes, Valentina only had half of what we needed. Italians have long been the world's specialists in revenge. Wilbur says that Allegra's was the fiercest and most beautiful materialization he has ever seen."

"Impressed me."

We sipped some more.

"Also, Shy, I think I'm gradually becoming you in certain ways."

"How?"

"Loving you has Christianized me to a degree. And that's been a surprise."

"Really? You mean you're going to take me and our children to church?"

"Let's not get ahead of ourselves. But you know, Crowley was never anything but a ghost. His life was a ghost's life, the Ghost of Christianity Past. The Satanism, the Faustian pacts, the demon conjuring, the old traditions of black magic. He represented discarded possibilities that had left their sediment across the Christian centuries. Our battle against him was in essence an ancient battle against sin. There's only one way to win a battle like that. Goodness! We couldn't have won it without your goodness. Look what you did with those sex dreams. *You made them good.*"

"I must be my mother's daughter. The devil made me do it. For me you made them *bad*—the fun kind of bad."

I gradually saw the implication. "Shy, we're becoming each other. . . ."

In this household we think complexities matter. But after airing the complexities, we can get real simple. We went to our beautiful new bedroom and made fools of ourselves.

230

Afterword

Almost all of the information in this book about Aleister Crowley and the Agape Lodge of the Pasadena OTO is historically accurate. Most of what isn't historical concerns the purely fictional movie Grady McMurtry commissions from Benedek Sarka.

Many of Crowley's books, including his poetry, are available in online archives. I made use of biographical details found in Richard Kaczynski's *Perdurabo: The Life of Aleister Crowley* (North Altantic Books, 2010), John Symonds's *The Magic of Aleister Crowley* (CreateSpace, 2014), and Colin Wilson's *Aleister Crowley: The Nature of the Beast* (Aeon, 2005). I also consulted an unusually scholarly and well-documented graphic novel, *Aleister Crowley: Wandering the Waste* (Markosia Enterprises, 2013), by Martin Hayes. For Crowley's place in intellectual history, see Hugh B. Urban's *Magia Sexualis: Sex, Magic, and Liberation in Modern Western Esotericism* (University of California Press, 2006). The sorcerer did in fact have a hard time in the Sahara Desert with a defiant demon named Choronzon, originally conjured in Elizabethan times by Edward Kelley and John Dee. I believe that I am the first to relate Crowley's Choronzon to figures Milton's Satan encounters at the court of Chaos in *Paradise Lost*.

There is controversy over the magus's last words. One candidate is "I am perplexed." Perhaps this utterance appeals to some Crowley enthusiasts because it is close in sound and meaning to Prospero's "Sir, I am vexed." At the end Crowley echoed his magical counterpart in Shakespeare. But I think the case for "Sometimes I hate myself" rests on stronger factual grounds, since the other story was reported to John Symonds by Lady Frieda Harris, who was not present at Netherworld when the magician died.

Peter Brook's first theatrical production, the Torch Theatre *Doctor Faustus* of 1942, occupies a key position in my plot. I gathered what little is known of its brief run from several sources, primarily Brook's own memoir, *Threads of Time* (Counterpoint, 1999).

I suspect that the influence of Crowley on subsequent culture, especially rock 'n roll, is wide but shallow. There are exceptions, however. Kenneth Anger and Jimmy Page are certainly serious disciples of Crowley, as was fellow drug enthusiast Timothy Leary. (One of Crowley's autobiographical potboilers is called *Confessions of a Drug Fiend*). The fullest discussion of these matters is Gary Lachman's *Aleister Crowley: Magick, Rock and Roll*, *and the Wickedest Man in the World* (Penguin, 2014). The author, formerly the bassist for Blondie, speaks from experience.

Two of the three rare films in the Sarka estate could possibly exist. The other, *Three Queens*, is my invention. One can learn a great deal more about that movie from my novel *Shooting in Universal City* (CreateSpace, 2015).

The story of Valentina Griswold and a ghost named Bernardino Herrera resides in *The Ghost Killers of Black Ash Canyon*, the first of my tales of the Ghost Killers. I am currently at work on a third installment.

The enchanting picture of Aleister Crowley on my front cover is the work of artist-scholar Marina Favila.

www.ingramcontent.com/pod-product-compliance
Lightning Source LLC
Chambersburg PA
CBHW051431170626
46809CB00006B/2418